Grandfather's Private Zoo

Ruskin Bond is known for his signature simplistic and witty writing style. He is the author of several bestselling short stories, novellas, collections, essays and children's books; and has contributed a number of poems and articles to various magazines and anthologies. At the age of twenty-three, he won the prestigious John Llewellyn Rhys Prize for his first novel, *The Room on the Roof.* He was also the recipient of the Padma Shri in 1999, Lifetime Achievement Award by the Delhi Government in 2012 and the Padma Bhushan in 2014.

Born in 1934, Ruskin Bond grew up in Jamnagar, Shimla, New Delhi and Dehradun. Apart from three years in the UK, he has spent all his life in India, and now lives in Landour, Mussoorie, with his adopted family.

RUSKIN BOND

Grandfather's Private Zoo

RUPA

Published by
Rupa Publications India Pvt. Ltd 2021
7/16, Ansari Road, Daryaganj
New Delhi 110002

Sales centres:
Allahabad Bengaluru Chennai
Hyderabad Jaipur Kathmandu
Kolkata Mumbai

ISBN: 978-93-5520-030-3

First impression 2021

10 9 8 7 6 5 4 3 2 1

Moral right of the author has been asserted.

CONTENTS

INTRODUCTION

Have you ever looked at an animal—your pet, a monkey on the street, a tiger on a safari—and wondered what is going on in its head? What kind of thoughts do animals have? Do they worry about their younglings? What do they think of humans? Are we just an annoyance that they have learnt to live with? Or are they also curious about the way humans function?

The animal world offers us many wonders; we often look on in awe at the majestic animals of the forest, or look at our pets and wonder how we were lucky enough to have gotten such a pure creature. Animals and humans can form unique bonds that last a lifetime; they help each other travel through life in myriad ways. Animals enrich the human experience.

This book explores exactly this equation between animals and humans, and tells us tales of loyalty, adventure and mischief. Whether it be the tale of a monkey with an affinity for pearls; a crow that observes and sings about the humans around him; or of uncle and nephew going on adventures to the forest.

This collection of stories and personal essays is for children and adults alike—the only prerequisite to read this book is love for and curiosity about the creatures we find in nature!

Ruskin Bond

THE ADVENTURES OF TOTO

Grandfather bought Toto from a tonga-driver for a sum of five rupees. The tonga-driver used to keep the little red monkey tied to a feeding trough, and the monkey looked so out of place there that Grandfather decided he would add the little fellow to his private zoo.

Toto was a pretty monkey. His bright eyes sparkled with mischief beneath deep-set eyebrows, and his teeth, which were a pearly white, were very often displayed in a smile that frightened the life out of elderly Anglo-Indian ladies. But his hands looked dried-up as though they had been pickled in the sun for many years. Yet his fingers were quick and wicked; and his tail, while adding to his good looks (Grandfather believed a tail would add to anyone's good looks), also served as a third hand. He could use it to hang from a branch; and it was capable of scooping up any delicacy that might be out of reach of his hands.

Grandmother always fussed when Grandfather brought home some new bird or animal. So it was decided that Toto's presence should be kept a secret from her until she was in a particularly good mood. Grandfather and I put him away in a little closet opening into my bedroom wall, where he was tied securely—or so we thought—to a peg fastened into the wall.

A few hours later, when Grandfather and I came back to release Toto, we found that the walls, which had been covered with some ornamental paper chosen by Grandfather, now stood out as naked brick and plaster. The peg in the wall had been wrenched from its socket, and my school blazer, which had been hanging there, was in shreds. I wondered what Grandmother would say. But Grandfather didn't worry; he seemed pleased with Toto's performance.

'He's clever,' said Grandfather. 'Given time, I'm sure he could have tied the torn pieces of your blazer into a rope, and made his escape from the window!'

His presence in the house still a secret, Toto was now transferred to a big cage in the servants' quarters where a number of Grandfather's pets lived very sociably together—a tortoise, a pair of rabbits, a tame squirrel and, for a while, my pet goat. But the monkey wouldn't allow any of his companions to sleep at night; so Grandfather, who had to leave Dehradun the next day to collect his pension in Saharanpur, decided to take him along.

Unfortunately, I could not accompany Grandfather on that trip, but he told me about it afterwards. A big black canvas kitbag was provided for Toto. This, with some straw at the bottom, became his new abode. When the strings of the bag were tied, there was no escape. Toto could not get his hands through the opening, and the canvas was too strong for him to bite his way through. His efforts to get out only had the effect of making the bag roll about on the floor or occasionally jump into the air—an exhibition that attracted a curious crowd of onlookers on the Dehradun railway platform.

Toto remained in the bag as far as Saharanpur, but while Grandfather was producing his ticket at the railway turnstile, Toto suddenly poked his head out of the bag and gave the ticket collector a wide grin.

The poor man was taken aback; but, with great presence of mind and much to Grandfather's annoyance, he said, 'Sir, you have a dog with you. You'll have to pay for it accordingly.'

In vain did Grandfather take Toto out of the bag; in vain did he try to prove that a monkey did not qualify as a dog, or even as a quadruped. Toto was classified a dog by the ticket collector; and three rupees was the sum handed over as his fare. Then Grandfather, just to get his own back, took from his pocket our pet tortoise, and said, 'What must I pay for this, since you charge for all animals?'

The ticket collector looked closely at the tortoise, prodded it with his forefinger, gave Grandfather a pleased and triumphant look, and said, 'No charge. It is not a dog.'

When Toto was finally accepted by Grandmother, he was given a comfortable home in the stable, where he had for a companion the family donkey, Nana. On Toto's first night in the stable, Grandfather paid him a visit to see if he was comfortable. To his surprise he found Nana, without apparent cause, pulling at her tether and trying to keep her head as far as possible from a bundle of hay.

Grandfather gave Nana a slap across her haunches, and she jerked back, dragging Toto with her. He had fastened on to her long ears with his sharp little teeth.

Toto and Nana never became friends.

A great treat for Toto during cold winter evenings was the large bowl of warm water given to him by Grandmother for his bath. He would cunningly test the temperature with his hand, then gradually step into the bath, first one foot, then the other (as he had seen me doing), until he was in the water up to his neck. Once comfortable, he would take the soap in his hands or feet, and rub himself all over. When the water became cold, he would get out, and run as quickly as he could to the kitchen fire in order to dry himself. If anyone laughed at him during this performance, Toto's feelings would be hurt and he would refuse to go on with his bath.

One day Toto nearly succeeded in boiling himself alive.

A large kitchen kettle had been left on the fire to boil for tea. And Toto, finding himself with nothing better to do, decided to remove the lid. Finding the water just warm enough for a bath, he got in, with his head sticking out from the open kettle, This was just fine for a while, until the water began to boil. Toto then raised himself a little; but, finding it cold outside, sat down again. He continued hopping up and down for some time, until Grandmother arrived and hauled him, half-boiled, out of the kettle.

If there is a part of the brain especially devoted to mischief, that part was largely developed in Toto. He was always tearing things to pieces. Whenever one of my aunts came near him, he made every effort to get hold of her dress and tear a hole in it.

One day, at lunchtime, a large dish of pulao rice stood in the centre of the dining table. We entered the room to find Toto stuffing himself with rice. My grandmother screamed—and Toto threw a plate at her. One of my aunts rushed forward and received a glass of water in the face. When Grandfather arrived, Toto picked up the dish of pulao and made his exit through a window. We found him in the branches of the jackfruit tree, the dish still in his arms. He remained there all afternoon, eating slowly through the rice, determined on finishing every grain. And then, in order to spite Grandmother, who had screamed at him, he threw the dish down from the tree, and chattered with delight when it broke into a hundred pieces.

Obviously Toto was not the sort of pet we could keep for long. Even Grandfather realized that. We were not well-to-do, and could not afford the frequent loss of dishes, clothes, curtains and wallpaper. So Grandfather found the tonga-driver, and sold Toto back to him—for only three rupees.

THE CONCEITED PYTHON

There was one pet which Grandfather could not keep for very long. Grandmother was tolerant of some birds and animals, but she drew the line at reptiles. Even a chameleon as sweet-tempered as Henry (we will come to him later) made her blood run cold. Grandfather should have known that there was little chance of being allowed to keep a python.

He never could resist buying unusual pets, and while we still had Toto, he paid a snake charmer in the bazaar only four rupees for the young four-foot python that was on display to a crowd of eager boys and girls. Grandfather impressed the gathering by slinging the python over his shoulders and walking home with it.

The first to see them arrive was Toto, swinging from a branch of the jackfruit tree. One look at the python, ancient enemy of his race, and he fled into the house, squealing with fright. The noise brought Grandmother on to the veranda, where she nearly fainted at the sight of the python curled around Grandfather's neck.

'It will strangle you to death,' she cried. 'Get rid of it at once!'

'Nonsense!' said Grandfather. 'He's only a young fellow—he'll soon get used to us.'

'He might, indeed,' said Grandmother, 'but I have no intention of getting used to him. And you know your cousin Mabel is coming to stay with us tomorrow. She'll leave the minute she knows there's a snake in the house.'

'Well, perhaps we should show it to her as soon as she arrives,' said Grandfather, who did not look forward to the visits of relatives any more than I did.

'You'll do no such thing,' said Grandmother.

'Well, I can't let it loose in the garden. It might find its way into the poultry house and then where would we be?'

'Oh, how irritating you are!' grumbled Grandmother. 'Lock the thing in the bathroom, then go out and find the man you bought it from, and get him to come here and collect it.'

And so, in my awestruck presence, Grandfather took the python into the bathroom and placed it in the tub. After closing the door on it, he gave me a sad look.

'Perhaps Grandmother is right this time,' he said. 'After all, we don't want the snake to get hold of Toto. And it's sure to be very hungry.'

He hurried off to the bazaar to look for the snake charmer, and was gone for about two hours, while Grandmother paced up and down the veranda. When Grandfather returned, looking crestfallen, we knew he had not been able to find the snake charmer.

'Well, then, kindly take it away yourself,' said Grandmother. 'Leave it in the jungle across the riverbed.'

'All right, but let me feed it first,' said Grandfather. He

produced a plucked chicken (in those days you could get a chicken for less than a rupee), and went into the bathroom, followed, in single file, by myself, Grandmother, and the cook and gardener.

Grandfather opened the door and stepped into the room. I peeped around his legs, while the others stayed well behind. We could not see the python anywhere.

'He's gone,' announced Grandfather.

'He couldn't have gone far,' said Grandmother. 'Look under the tub.'

We looked under the tub, but the python was not there. Then Grandfather went to the window. 'We left it open,' he said. 'He must have gone this way.'

A careful search was made of the house, the kitchen, the garden, the stable and the poultry shed; but the python could not be found anywhere.

'He must have gone over the garden wall,' said Grandfather. 'He'll be well away by now.'

'I certainly hope so,' said Grandmother, with a look of relief.

Aunt Mabel arrived the next day for a three-week visit and for a couple of days Grandfather and I were a little worried in case the python made a sudden appearance; but on the third day, when he did not show up, we felt sure that he had gone for good.

And then, towards evening, we were startled by a scream from the garden. Seconds later Aunt Mabel came flying up the veranda steps, looking as though she had seen the devil himself.

'In the guava tree!' she gasped. 'I was reaching for a guava when I saw it staring at me. The look in its eyes! As though it would eat me alive...'

'Calm down, my dear,' urged Grandmother, sprinkling eau de cologne over my aunt. 'Tell us, what did you see?'

'A snake!' sobbed Aunt Mabel. 'A great boa constrictor. It must have been twenty feet long! In the guava tree. Its eyes were terrible. And it looked at me in such a queer way...'

My grandparents exchanged glances and Grandfather said, 'I'll go out and kill it.' Taking hold of an umbrella, he sallied forth into the garden. But when he got to the guava tree, the python had gone.

'Aunt Mabel must have frightened it away,' I said.

'Hush,' said Grandfather. 'We mustn't speak of your aunt in that way.' But his eyes were alive with laughter.

After this incident, the python began to make a number of appearances, always in the most unexpected places. Aunt Mabel had another fit when she saw him emerge from beneath a cushion. She packed her bags and left.

The hunt continued.

One morning I saw the python curled up on the dressing table, gazing at his own reflection in the mirror. I went for Grandfather, but by the time we returned to the room the python had moved on. He was seen in the garden and once the cook saw him crawling up the iron ladder to the roof. Then we found him on the dressing table a second time, admiring himself in the mirror. Evidently he was fascinated by his own reflection.

'All the attention he's getting has probably made him conceited,' said Grandfather.

'He's trying to look better for Aunt Mabel,' I said. (I regretted this remark because Grandmother overheard and held up my pocket money for the rest of the week.)

'Anyway, now we know his weakness,' said Grandfather.

'Are *you* trying to be funny too?' said Grandmother.

'I didn't mean Aunt Mabel,' explained Grandfather. 'The python is becoming vain, so it should be easier to catch him.'

Grandfather set about preparing a large cage, with a mirror at one end. In the cage he left a juicy chicken and several other tasty things. The opening was fitted up with a trapdoor.

Aunt Mabel had already left by the time we set up the trap, but we had to go on with the project because we could not have the python prowling about the house indefinitely. A python's bite is not poisonous, but it can swallow a live monkey, and it can be a risky playmate for a small boy.

For a few days nothing happened; and then, as I was leaving for school one morning, I saw the python in the cage. He had eaten everything left out for him, and was curled in front of the mirror, with something that resembled a smile on his face—if you can imagine a python smiling.

I lowered the trapdoor gently, but the python took no notice of me. Grandfather and the gardener put the cage in a tonga and took it across the riverbed. Opening the trapdoor, they left the cage in the jungle. When they went away, the python had made no attempt to get out.

'I didn't have the heart to take the mirror away from him,' said Grandfather. 'It's the first time I've seen a snake fall in love.'

A HORNBILL CALLED HAROLD

Harold's mother, like all good hornbills, was the most careful of wives; his father, the most easy-going of husbands. In January before the dhak tree burst into flame-red blossom, Harold's father took his wife into a giant hole high in the tree trunk, where his father and father's father had taken their brides at the same time every year. In this weather-beaten hollow, generation upon generation of hornbills had been raised; and Harold's mother, like those before her, was enclosed within the hole by a sturdy wall of earth, sticks, and dung.

Harold's father left a small slit in the centre of this wall, to enable him to communicate with his wife whenever he felt like a chat. Walled up in her uncomfortable room, Harold's mother was a prisoner for over two months. During this period an egg was laid, and Harold was born.

In his naked boyhood Harold was no beauty. His most prominent feature was his flaming red bill, matching the blossoms of the flame tree which were now ablaze, heralding the summer. He had a stomach that could never be filled, despite the best efforts of his parents, who brought him pieces of jackfruit and berries from the banyan tree.

As he grew bigger, the room became more cramped and one day his mother burst through the wall, spread out her wings, and sailed over the treetops. Her husband pretended he was glad to see her about and played with her, expressing his delight with deep gurgles and throaty chuckles. Then they repaired the wall of the nursery, so that Harold would not fall out.

Harold was quite happy in his cell, and felt no urge for freedom. He was putting on weight and feathers and acquiring a philosophy of his own. Then something happened to change the course of his life.

One afternoon he was awakened from his siesta by a loud banging on the wall, a banging quite different from that made by his parents. Soon the wall gave way, and there was something large and red staring at him—not his parents' bills, but Grandfather's sunburnt face and short red beard.

In a moment Harold was seized. He roared lustily and struck out with his bill and feet, but to no purpose. Grandfather had him in a bag, and the young hornbill was added to the zoo on our front veranda.

Harold had a simple outlook and once he had got over some early attacks of nerves, he began to welcome the approach of strangers. For him, Grandfather and I meant the arrival of food, and he greeted us with craning neck, quivering open bill and a loud, croaking '*Ka-Ka-Kaee!*' Grandfather gave him a very roomy cage in a sunny corner of the veranda—a palace compared to the cramped quarters he had grown up in—and a basin of fresh water every day for his bath.

Harold was not beautiful by Indian standards. He had a

small body and a large head. But his nature was friendly and he stayed on good terms with both my grandparents during his twelve years as a member of the household. He would even tolerate my aunts, to whom most of the other pets in the house usually took a strong dislike.

Harold's best friends were those who fed him, and he was willing even to share his food with us, sometimes trying to feed me with his great beak. Eating was a serious business for Harold, and if there was any delay at mealtimes he would summon us with raucous barks and vigorous bangs of his bill on the woodwork of his cage.

He loved bananas and dates and balls of boiled rice. I would throw him the rice-balls, and he would catch them in his beak, toss them into the air, and let them drop into his open mouth. He perfected his trick of catching things and Grandfather trained him to catch a tennis ball thrown with some force from a distance of fifteen yards. Harold would have made an excellent slip fielder at cricket.

Having no family, profession or religion, Harold gave much time and thought to his personal appearance. He carried a rouge-pot on his person and used it very skilfully as an item of his morning toilet. This rouge-pot was a small gland situated above the roots of his tail feathers; it produced a rich yellow fluid. Harold would dip into his rouge-pot from time to time and then rub the colour over his feathers and the back of his neck. The colour came off on one's hands when one touched Harold. I think his colour had some sort of waterproofing effect because he used his colour-pot most during the rains.

Harold never drank anything, not even water, in all the

years he stayed with Grandfather. Apparently hornbills get all the liquid they need from their solid food.

Only once did he misbehave. That was when he removed a lighted cigar from the hand of an American friend who was visiting us and swallowed it. It was a moving experience for Harold and an unnerving one for our guest. Both had to be given some brandy.

Though Harold drank no water, he loved the rain. We always knew when it was going to rain, because Harold would start chuckling to himself about one hour before the raindrops fell. This used to irritate my aunts. They were always being caught in the rain. Harold would be chuckling when they left the house; and when they returned drenched to the skin, he would be in fits of laughter.

As the storm clouds gathered, and gusts of wind shook the banana trees, Harold would get very excited, and his chuckle would change to an eerie whistle. '*Wheee...wheee*' he would scream. And then, as the first drops of rain hit the veranda steps, and the scent of the freshened earth passed through the house, he would start roaring again like a drunk. The wind swept the rain into his spacious cage, and Harold would spread out his wings and dance, tumbling about like a circus clown.

When the monsoon really set in, he would get used to the rains, and his enthusiasm, like our own, would lessen. But the first few showers were always a wonder to him and we would come out on the veranda to watch him and share in his pleasure.

I miss Harold's raucous bark, and the banging of his great bill. If there is a heaven for good hornbills, I hope he is getting all the summer showers he could wish for and plenty of tennis balls to catch.

A LITTLE WORLD OF MUD

I had never thought there was much to be found in the rainwater pond behind our house except for quantities of mud and the occasional water buffalo. It was Grandfather who introduced me to the pond's diversity of life, so beautifully arranged that each individual gained some benefit from the well-being of the mass. To the inhabitants of the pond, the pond was the world; and to the inhabitants of the world, commented Grandfather, the world was but a muddy pond.

When Grandfather first showed me the pond world, he chose a dry place in the shade of an old peepul tree, where we sat for an hour, gazing steadily at the thin green scum on the water. The buffaloes had not arrived for their afternoon dip, the surface of the pond was undisturbed.

For the first ten minutes we saw nothing. Then a small black blob appeared in the middle of the pond. Gradually it rose higher until at last we could make out a frog's head, its big eyes staring hard at us. He did not know if we were friend or enemy and kept his body out of sight. A heron, his mortal enemy, might have been wading about in search of him. When he had made sure that we were not herons, he passed this information to his friends and neighbours, and very soon there were a number of big heads and eyes on the surface of the water. Throats swelled, and there began a chorus which went, '*wurk, wurk, wurk...*'

In the shallow water near the tree we could see a dark, shifting shadow. When we touched it with the end of a stick, the dark mass immediately became alive. Thousands of little black tadpoles wriggled into life, pushing and hustling one another.

'What do tadpoles eat?' I asked Grandfather.

'They eat one another much of the time,' said Grandfather, who had once kept a few in an aquarium. 'It may seem an unpleasant custom, but when you think of the thousands of tadpoles that are hatched, you will realize what a useful system it is. If all the young tadpoles in this pond became frogs, they would take up every inch of ground between us and the house!'

'Their croaking would certainly drive Grandmother crazy,' I said, to which Grandfather agreed.

When Grandfather was younger, he had once brought home a number of green tree frogs. He put them in a glass jar and left them on a windowsill without telling anyone, anyone at all, of their presence.

At about four in the morning the entire household was awakened by a loud and fearful noise, and Grandmother and several nervous relatives gathered on the veranda for safety. Their fear turned to anger when they discovered the source of the noise. At the first glimmer of dawn, the frogs had with one accord burst into song. Grandmother wanted to throw the frogs, bottle and all, out of the window, but Grandfather gave the bottle a good shaking, and the frogs stayed quiet. Everyone went to sleep again but Grandfather was obliged to stay awake in order to shake the bottle whenever the frogs showed signs of bursting into song again.

Fortunately for all concerned, the next day Aunt Mabel took the top off the bottle to see what was inside. The sight of a dozen green tree frogs so frightened her that she ran off without replacing the cover, and the frogs jumped out and got loose in the garden and were never seen again.

Their escape ruined Grandfather's project of using the tree frogs as barometers. His idea was to place the frogs in tall bottles with wooden ladders. The steps of the ladder would act as degree-marks. The frogs would climb to the top in fine weather but keep to the bottom of the bottle in bad weather. It was Grandfather's plan to consult his frogs before going out on picnics.

But to return to my own pond...

I soon grew into the habit of visiting it on my own, to explore its banks and shallows; and, taking off my shoes, I would wade into the muddy water up to my knees and pluck the water lilies off the surface.

One day, when I reached the pond, I found it already occupied by the buffaloes. Their owner, a boy a little older than I, was swimming about in the middle of the pond. Instead of climbing out on to the bank, he would pull himself up on the back of one of his buffaloes, stretch his naked brown body out on the animal's glistening back and start singing to himself.

When the boy saw me staring at him from across the pond, he smiled, showing gleaming white teeth in his dark, sunburnt face. He invited me to join him for a swim. I told him I could not swim and he offered to teach me. He dived off the back of his buffalo and swam across to me. And I, having removed my shirt and shorts, followed his instructions until I was struggling about among the water lilies.

The boy's name was Ramu, and he promised to give me swimming lessons every afternoon. And so it was during the afternoons—especially summer afternoons when everyone else was asleep—that we met.

Very soon I was able to swim across the pond to sit with Ramu astride a contented buffalo, standing like an island in the middle of a muddy ocean. Ramu came from a family of farmers and had as yet received no schooling. But he was well-versed in folklore and knew a great deal about birds and animals,

I liked the buffaloes too. Sometimes we would try racing them, Ramu and I riding on different buffaloes. But they were lazy creatures, and would leave one comfortable spot only for another or, if they were in no mood for games, would roll over on their backs, taking us with them into the mud and green scum of the pond. I would often emerge from the pond in shades of green and khaki, then slip into the house through the bathroom, bathing under the tap before getting into my clothes.

Ramu and I sat on our favourite buffalo and watched a pair of sarus cranes prancing and capering around each other: tall, stork-like birds with naked red heads and long red legs. They are always very devoted companions, and it is said that if a sarus is killed its mate will haunt the scene for weeks, calling sadly, and sometimes pining away and dying of grief. They are held in great affection by village people, and when caught young, make excellent pets. Though Grandfather did not keep a sarus crane, he said they were as good as watchdogs, giving loud trumpet-like calls when they were disturbed.

'Many birds are sacred,' said Ramu, as a blue jay swooped down from the peepul tree and carried off a grasshopper. He told me that both the blue jay and Lord Shiva were called Nilkanth. Shiva had a blue throat, like the bird, because out of compassion for the human race, he had swallowed a deadly poison meant to destroy the world. Keeping the poison in his throat, he did not let it go down any further.

'Are squirrels sacred?' I asked.

'Lord Rama loved squirrels,' said Ramu. 'He would take them in his arms and stroke them with his long fingers. That is why they have four dark lines down their backs from head to tail. The lines are the marks of his fingers.'

It seemed that both Ramu and Grandfather were of the opinion that we should be more gentle with birds and animals, and not kill so many of them.

'It is also important that we respect them,' said Grandfather. 'We must acknowledge their rights on the earth. Everywhere, birds and animals are finding it more difficult to live because we are destroying their forests. They have to keep moving as the trees disappear.'

Ramu and I spent many long summer afternoons at the pond. Only the buffaloes and the frogs and the sarus cranes knew of our friendship. They had accepted us as part of their own world, their muddy but comfortable pond. And when finally I went away, both they and Ramu must have assumed that I would return like the birds.

THE BANYAN TREE

Though the house and grounds belonged to my grandparents, the magnificent old banyan tree was mine—chiefly because Grandfather, at sixty-five, could no longer climb it.

Its spreading branches, which hung to the ground and took root again, forming a number of twisting passages, gave me endless pleasure. Among them were squirrels and snails and butterflies. The tree was older than the house, older than Grandfather, as old as Dehradun itself. I could hide myself in its branches, behind thick green leaves, and spy on the world below.

My first friend was a small grey squirrel. Arching his back and sniffing into the air, he seemed at first to resent my invasion of his privacy. But when he found that I did not arm myself with catapult or airgun, he became friendly, and when I started bringing him pieces of cake and biscuit, he grew quite bold and was soon taking morsels from my hand.

Before long he was delving into my pockets and helping himself to whatever he could find. He was a very young squirrel and his friends and relatives probably thought him foolish and headstrong for trusting a human.

In the spring, when the banyan tree was full of small red figs, birds of all kinds would flock into its branches: the red-bottomed bulbul, cheerful and greedy; gossipy rosy pastors; parrots, mynahs and crows squabbling with one another. During the fig season, the banyan tree was the noisiest place in the garden.

Halfway up the tree I had built a crude platform where I would spend the afternoons when it was not too hot. I could read there, propping myself up against the bole of the tree with a cushion from the living room. *Treasure Island, The Adventures of Huckleberry Finn* and *The Story of Doctor Dolittle* were some of the books that made up my banyan tree library.

When I did not feel like reading, I could look down through the leaves at the world below. And, on one particular afternoon, I had a grandstand view of that classic of the Indian wilds, a fight between a mongoose and a cobra. And this one had not been staged for my benefit!

The warm breezes of approaching summer had sent everyone, including the gardener, into the house. I was feeling drowsy myself, wondering if I should go to the pond and have a swim with Ramu and the buffaloes, when I saw a huge black cobra gliding out of a clump of cactus. At the same time a mongoose emerged from the bushes and went straight for the cobra.

In a clearing beneath the banyan tree, in bright sunshine, they came face to face.

The cobra knew only too well that the grey mongoose, three feet long, was a superb fighter, clever and aggressive. But the cobra, too, was a skilful and experienced fighter. He could move swiftly and strike with the speed of light; and the sacs behind his long, sharp fangs were full of deadly poison.

It was to be a battle of champions.

Hissing defiance, his forked tongue darting in and out, the cobra raised three of his six feet off the ground and spread his spectacled hood. The mongoose bushed his tail. The long hair on his spine stood up.

Though the combatants were unaware of my presence in the tree, they were soon made aware of the arrival of two other spectators. One was a mynah, the other a jungle crow. They had seen these preparations for battle and had settled on the cactus to watch the outcome. Had they been content only to watch, all would have been well with both of them.

The cobra stood on the defensive, swaying slowly from side to side, trying to mesmerize the mongoose into making a false move. But the mongoose knew the power of his opponent's glassy, unwinking eyes, and refused to meet them. Instead, he fixed his gaze at a point just below the cobra's hood and opened the attack.

Moving forward quickly, until he was just within the cobra's reach, the mongoose made a pretended move to one side. Immediately the cobra struck. His great hood came down so swiftly that I thought nothing could save the mongoose. But the little fellow jumped neatly to one side, and darted in as swiftly as the cobra, biting the snake on the back and darting away again out of reach.

At the same moment that the cobra struck, the crow and the mynah hurled themselves at him, only to collide heavily in mid-air. Shrieking insults at each other, they returned to the cactus plant.

A few drops of blood glistened on the cobra's back. The

cobra struck again and missed. Again the mongoose sprang aside, jumped in and bit. Again, the birds dived at the snake, bumped into each other instead and returned shrieking to the safety of the cactus.

The third round followed the same course as the first two with one dramatic difference. The crow and the mynah, determined to take part in the proceedings, dived at the snake but this time they missed each other as well as their mark. The mynah flew on and reached its perch, but the crow tried to pull up in mid-air and turn back. In the second that it took the bird to do this, the cobra whipped his head back and struck with great force, his snout thudding against the crow's body.

I saw the bird flung nearly twenty feet across the garden. It fluttered about for a while, then lay still. The mynah remained on the cactus plant, and when the snake and the mongoose returned to the fight, very wisely decided not to interfere again!

The cobra was weakening, and the mongoose, walking fearlessly up to it, raised himself on his short legs and with a lightning snap had the big snake by the snout. The cobra writhed and lashed about in a frightening manner, and even coiled itself about the mongoose, but to no avail. The little fellow hung grimly on, until the snake had ceased to struggle. He then smelt it along its quivering length, gripped it round the hood and dragged it into the bushes.

The mynah dropped cautiously to the ground, hopped about, jeered into the bushes from a safe distance, and then, with a shrill cry of congratulation, flew away.

The banyan tree was also the setting for what we were to call the Strange Case of the Grey Squirrel and the White Rat.

The white rat was Grandfather's—he had bought it for one-quarter of a rupee but I would often take it with me into the banyan tree, where it soon struck up a friendship with one of the squirrels. They would go off together on little excursions among the roots and branches of the old tree.

Then the squirrel started building a nest. At first she tried building it in my pockets, and when I went indoors and took off my clothes I would find straw and grass falling out.

Then one day Grandmother's knitting was missing. We hunted for it everywhere but without success.

The next day I saw something glinting in a hole in the tree. Going up to investigate, I saw that it was the end of Grandmother's steel knitting needle. On looking further, I discovered that the hole was crammed with knitting. Amongst the wool were three baby squirrels—and all of them were white!

We gazed at the white squirrels in wonder and fascination. Grandfather was puzzled at first, but when I told him about the white rat's visits to the tree, his brow cleared. He said the white rat must be the father.

A CROW IN THE HOUSE

The young crow had fallen from its nest and was fluttering about on the road, in danger of being crushed by a cart or a tonga, or seized by a cat, when I picked it up and brought it home. It was in a sorry condition, beak gaping and head dropping, and we did not expect it to live. But Grandfather and I did our best to bring it around. We fed it by prising its beak gently open with a pencil, pushing in a little bread and milk, then removing the pencil to allow it to swallow. We varied its diet with occasional doses of Grandmother's home-made wine, and as a result the young crow was soon on the road to recovery.

He was offered his freedom but he did not take it. Instead he made himself at home in the house. Grandmother, Aunt Mabel, and even some of Grandfather's pets objected; but there was no way of getting rid of the bird. He took over the administration of the house.

We were not sure that he was male, but we called him Caesar.

Before long, Caesar was joining us at mealtimes, besides his own grubs or beetles in the garden. He danced on the dining table and gave us no peace until he had been given his small bowl of meat and soup and vegetables. He was always restless, fidgeting about, investigating things. He would hop across a table to empty a matchbox of its contents, or rip the daily paper to shreds, or overturn a vase of flowers, or tug at the tail of one of the dogs.

'That crow will be the ruin of us!' grumbled Grandmother, picking marigolds off the carpet. 'Can't you keep him in a cage?'

We did try keeping Caesar in a cage, but he was so angry, and objected with such fierce cawing and flapping, that it was better for our nerves and peace of mind to give him the run of the house. He did not show any inclination to join the other crows in the banyan tree. Grandfather said this was because he was really a jungle crow—a raven of sorts—and probably felt a little contemptuous of very ordinary carrion crows. But it seemed to me that Caesar, having grown used to living with humans on equal terms, had become snobbish and did not wish to mix with his own kind. He would even squabble with Harold the hornbill. Perching on Harold's cage, he would peck at the big bird's feet, whereupon Harold would swear and scold and try to catch Caesar through the bars.

In time, Caesar learnt to talk a little—as ravens sometimes do—in a cracked, throaty voice. He would sit for hours outside the window, banging on the glass with his beak, and calling, '*Hello, hello.*' He seemed to recognize the click of the gate when I came home from school, and would come to the door with a hop, skip and jump, saying, '*Hello, hello!*' I had also taught him to sit on my arm and say '*Kiss, kiss*', while he placed his head gently against my mouth.

On one of Aunt Mabel's visits, Caesar alighted on her

and cackled, '*Kiss, kiss!*' Aunt Mabel was delighted—possibly flattered—and leant forward for a kiss. But Caesar's attention shifted to my aunt's gleaming spectacles, and thrusting at them with his beak, he knocked them off. Aunt Mabel never was a success with the pets.

Pet or pest? Grandmother insisted that Caesar was a pest, in spite of his engaging habits. If he had restricted his activities to our own house, it would not have been so bad; but he took to visiting neighbouring houses and stealing pens and pencils, hair-ribbons, combs, keys, shuttlecocks, toothbrushes and false teeth. He was especially fond of toothbrushes, and made a collection of them on top of the cupboard in my room. Most of the neighbours were represented in our house by a toothbrush. Toothbrush sales went up that year. So did Grandmother's blood pressure.

Caesar spied on children going into the bania's shop, and often managed to snatch sweets from them as they came out. Clothes pegs fascinated him. Neighbours would return from the bazaar to find their washing lying in the mud and no sign of the pegs. These, too, found their way to the top of my cupboard.

It was Caesar's gardening activities that finally led to disaster. He was helping himself to our neighbour's beans when a stick was flung at him, breaking his leg. I carried the unfortunate bird home, and Grandfather and I washed and bandaged his leg as best we could. But it would not mend. Caesar hung his head and no longer talked. He grew weaker day by day, refusing to eat. An occasional sip of Grandmother's home-made wine was all that kept him going.

One morning I found him dead on the sofa, his legs stiff

in the air. Poor Caesar! His anti-social habits had led to his early end.

I dug a shallow grave in the garden, and buried him there, along with all the toothbrushes and clothes pegs he had taken so much trouble to collect.

HENRY: A CHAMELEON

This is the story of Henry, our pet chameleon. Chameleons are in a class by themselves and are no ordinary reptiles. From their nearest relatives, the lizards, they are easily distinguished by certain outstanding marks. Henry's tongue was as long as his body. On his head was a rigid crest which looked like a fireman's helmet. His limbs were long and slender and his fingers and toes were more developed than those of other reptiles.

Henry's most remarkable characteristics were his eyes. They were not beautiful. But his left eye was quite independent of his right. He could move one eye without disturbing the other. This gave him a horrible squint. Each eyeball, raised out of his head, was wobbled up and down, backwards and forwards, quite independently of its partner. Reptiles are not gifted like us with binocular vision. They do not see an object with both eyes at once.

Whenever I visited Henry, he would treat me with great caution, sitting perfectly still on his perch with his back to me, but his nearest eye would move around like the beam of a searchlight until it had got me well in focus. Then it would stop and the other eye would proceed to carry out an independent survey of its own in some different direction. Henry took nobody on trust, and treated my friendliest gestures with grave suspicion.

Tiring of his attitude, I would tickle him gently in the ribs with my finger. This always threw him into a great rage. He would blow himself up to an enormous size, his lungs filling his body with air. He would sit up on his hind legs, swaying from side to side, hoping to overawe me. Opening his mouth very wide, he would let out an angry hiss. But his protests went no further. He did not bite. Non-violence was his creed.

Many people believe the chameleon is a dangerous and poisonous reptile. When Grandfather was visiting a friend in the country, he came upon a noisy scene at the garden gate. Men were shouting, hurling stones, and brandishing sticks. The cause of all this was a chameleon who had been discovered sunning himself on a shrub. The gardener declared that it was a thing capable of poisoning people at a distance of twenty feet, and as a result the entire household had risen up in arms. Grandfather was in time to save the chameleon from certain death, and brought the little reptile home.

That chameleon was Henry and that was how he came to live with us.

Henry was a harmless creature. If I put my finger in his mouth, even in his wildest moments, he would simply wait for me to take it out again. I suppose he could bite. His rigid jaws carried a number of fine, pointed teeth. But Henry was rightly convinced that these were given to him solely for the purpose of chewing his food.

Provided I was patient, Henry was willing to take food from my hands. This he did very swiftly. His tongue was a sort of boomerang which came back to him with the food, an insect victim, attached to it. Before I could realize what had happened, the grasshopper held between my fingers would be lodged between Henry's jaws.

Henry did not cause any trouble in our house, but he did create something like a riot in the nursery school down the road.

It happened like this.

When the papayas in our garden were ripe, Grandmother usually sent a basket of them to her friend, Mrs Ghosh, who was the principal of the nursery school. On this occasion, Henry managed to smuggle himself into the basket of papayas when no one was looking. (He did have a cage of his own, but was seldom in it.) The gardener dutifully carried the papayas across to the school and left them in Mrs Ghosh's office. When Mrs Ghosh came in after making her rounds, she began admiring and examining the papayas. Out popped Henry.

Mrs Ghosh screamed. Henry would probably have liked to blush a deep red, but he turned a bright green instead, as that was the colour of the papayas. Mrs. Ghosh's assistant, Miss Daniels, rushed in, took one look at the chameleon, and joined in the screaming. Henry took fright and fled from the office, running down the corridor and into one of the classrooms. There he climbed on to a desk, while children ran in all directions, some to get away from Henry, some to catch him. But Henry made his exit from a window and disappeared in the garden.

Grandmother heard all about the incident from Mrs Ghosh but did not tell her the chameleon was ours. I did not think

Henry would find his way back to us, because the school was three houses away. But three days later, I found him sunning himself on the garden wall. He readily accepted some food from my hand and allowed himself to be recaptured.

A WEEK IN THE JUNGLE

Grandfather never hunted wild animals, he couldn't understand the pleasure some people obtained from killing the creatures of our forests. Birds and animals, he felt, had as much right to live as humans. We could kill them for food, he said, because even animals killed for food; but not for pleasure.

At the age of twelve I did not have the same high principles as Grandfather. Nevertheless, I disliked shooting. I found it boring.

Uncle Henry and some of his sporting friends once took me on a shikar expedition into the Terai jungles in the Shivalik range. The prospect of a week in the jungle, as camp-follower to several adults with guns, filled me with dismay. I knew that long, weary hours would be spent tramping behind these tall, professional-looking huntsmen who spoke in terms of bagging this tiger or that wild elephant, when all they ever got, if they were lucky, was a wild hare or a partridge. Tigers and excitement, it seemed, came only to Jim Corbett.

This particular expedition proved to be no different from others. There were four men with guns and at the end of the week all that they had shot were two miserable, underweight wildfowl. But I managed, on our second day in the jungle, to be left behind in the rest house. And, in the course of a morning's exploration of the old bungalow, I discovered a shelf of books half-hidden in a corner of the back veranda.

Who had left them there? A literary forest officer? A memsahib who had been bored by her husband's campfire boasting? Or someone who had no interest in the 'manly' sport of slaughtering wild animals and had brought his library along to pass the time? He must have left it behind for others like him.

Or possibly the poor fellow had gone into the jungle one day, as a gesture to his more bloodthirsty companions, and been trampled by an elephant, or gored by a wild boar, or (more likely) accidentally shot by one of the shikaris—and his sorrowing friends had taken his remains away and left his books behind.

Anyway, there they were—a shelf of some thirty volumes, in different shapes, sizes, and colours. I wiped the thick dust off the covers and examined the titles. As my reading tastes had not yet formed, I was willing to try anything. The bookshelf was varied in its contents—and my own interests have since remained fairly universal.

On that second day in the forest rest house, I discovered P. G. Wodehouse and read his *Love Among the Chickens*, an early Ukridge story and still one of my favourites. By the time the perspiring hunters came home in the evening, with their spent cartridges and impressive excuses, I had made a start with M. R. James's *Ghost Stories of an Antiquary*. This kept me awake most of the night, until the oil in the kerosene lamp was exhausted.

Next morning, fresh and optimistic again, the shikaris set out for a different area, where they hoped to get a tiger. They had employed a party of villagers to beat the jungle, and all day I could hear the tom-toms throbbing in the distance. This did not prevent me from finishing M. R. James, or discovering a little book called *A Naturalist on the Prowl* by 'E. H. A'. It described the tremendous fun and interest to be had from studying the wildlife in one's own back garden—the grasshoppers, beetles, ants, butterflies and praying mantises, all living such fascinating lives just outside (and sometimes inside) our bedroom windows.

Before I had finished the book, I was looking for spiders in the corners of the old bungalow and stalking grasshoppers in the long grass of the compound. My concentration was disturbed only once, when I looked up and saw a spotted deer crossing the open space in front of the house. The deer disappeared among the sal trees and I returned to the veranda and my book.

Dusk had fallen when I heard the party returning from the hunt. The hunters were talking loudly and seemed excited. Perhaps they had got their tiger. I put down my book and came out of the house to meet them.

'Did you get the tiger?' I asked excitedly.

'No, laddie,' said Uncle Henry. 'I think we'll get it tomorrow. You should have been with us—we saw a spotted deer!'

There were three days left and I knew I would never get through the entire bookshelf. This I did not intend doing, as not all the authors on the shelf appealed to me. I chose at random *The Wind in the Willows*, *The Jungle Book*, and *David Copperfield*.

On the day I made the literary acquaintance of Mowgli, the wolf-boy, the shikaris shot the two wildfowl already mentioned. As the party had from the first intended living off the jungle, only some tinned foods had been brought along; but two lean birds were insufficient for a party of five, and once again the meal consisted mostly of corned meat and mustard.

Next day, while the grown-ups were looking for their tiger and I was learning wisdom from the Water Rat, Toad, and other river people of *The Wind in the Willows*, an event took place which disturbed my reading for a little while.

I had noticed, on the previous day, that a number of stray mongrels—belonging to watchmen, villagers and forest-guards—always hung about the house, waiting for scraps of food to be thrown away. It was ten o'clock in the morning (a time when wild animals seldom come into the open), when I heard a sudden yelp in the clearing. Looking up, I saw a full-grown panther making off into the jungle with one of the dogs held in its mouth. The panther had either been driven towards the house by the beaters, or had watched the party leave the bungalow and decided to help itself to a meal.

There was no one else about at the time. Since the dog was obviously dead within seconds of being seized, and the panther had disappeared, I saw no point in raising an alarm but returned to my book.

It was getting late when the shikaris returned. They were dirty, sweaty and, as usual, disappointed. This time their excuses held a note of defiance. They took their corned meat in silence. Next day, we were to return to 'civilization', and none of the hunters had anything to show for a week in the jungles of India.

'No game left in these jungles,' said the leading member of the party, famed for once having shot two man-eating tigers and a basking crocodile in rapid succession.

'It's the weather,' said another. 'No rain at all this winter.'

'Don't know what the country's coming to,' grumbled the third.

'I saw a panther this morning,' I said modestly.

In fact, I was altogether too modest. I might just as well have said, 'I saw a donkey this morning,' for all the impression I made.

'Did you really?' said the leading hunter. He glanced at the book lying beside me. 'Young Master Copperfield says he saw a panther!'

The others were only faintly amused. They did not have the energy to laugh.

'Too imaginative for his age,' said one of them. 'Comes from reading so much, I suppose.'

'If you were to get out of the house and into the jungle a little,' said Uncle Henry reproachfully, 'you might really see a panther.'

'Don't know what young fellows are coming to these days...'

'Why didn't you grab it, man, and take it to Grandfather?' And everyone laughed.

I went to bed early and left them to their tales of the 'good old days' when rhinos, cheetahs, and possibly even the legendary phoenix were still available for slaughter.

I came home with a poor reputation. My uncle's friends thought I was both a sissy and a liar. And Uncle Henry, poor man, seemed to think I was responsible for the failure of the entire expedition. He did not take me with him again. But Grandfather, when I told him all about the hunt, doubled up with laughter and said he wished he had been with us, if only to see the faces of Uncle Henry and his friends. As a measure of his delight, he bought me a copy of *David Copperfield*, for I had not been able to finish the one in the forest rest house. I finally got through it in the banyan tree, in the company of several squirrels and a very noisy cicada.

A PHOTOGRAPH

Grandmother sat in a rocking chair, under the mango tree. It was late summer and there were sunflowers in the garden and a warm wind in the trees. Grandmother was knitting me a pullover for the winter months. Her hair was white, her eyes were not very strong, but her fingers moved quickly with the needles and the needles kept clicking all afternoon. Grandmother was old, but there were very few wrinkles on her skin.

In some of my tales I have perhaps been guilty of writing more admiringly of Grandfather than of Grandmother. It's true that Grandfather and I had much in common and that he gave me more of his time; but then, he had more time to give. He was a retired gentleman. But housewives never retire. And Grandmother always had housework. She saw to our meals, she did the shopping, kept the household accounts and dealt with a variety of tradesmen including the butcher, the baker, the dhobi and various egg, fruit, vegetable and charcoal vendors.

And so, if our pets sometimes hindered her in the efficient running of the house, who can blame her for being a little short with us at times?

In the long run, though Grandmother grumbled, she tolerated most of our pets. She nursed Toto the monkey when he was sick; she was fond of the hornbill; in fact, she liked all birds. She kept her own birdbath in the garden, where mynas, thrushes, bulbuls and flower-peckers would come for a dip or a drink, and she never forgot to fill the stone bath with fresh water in the mornings.

When she did find time to relax in her rocking chair, she liked having me beside her, and she liked talking about her youth.

One afternoon after lunch (or tiffin, as we called it then) I was rummaging in a box of old books and family heirlooms that I had found in the box room. There was not much to interest me except a book on butterflies, and as I was going through it I found a small photograph in between the pages. It was a faded picture, a little yellow and foggy—a picture of a girl standing against a wall; and from the other side of the wall a pair of hands reached up, as though someone were about climb over it. There were flowers growing near the girl, but I could not tell what they were; there was a small tree, too, but it was just a tree to me.

I ran out into the garden.

'Granny!' I shouted. 'Look at this picture! I found it in that box of old things. Whose picture is it?'

I raised myself on the arm of the rocking chair and we toppled over into a bed of nasturtiums.

'Now look what you've gone and done,' said Grandmother. 'I've lost count of my stitches. The next time you jump up like that, I'll make you finish the pullover yourself.'

Grandmother was always threatening to teach me how to knit. She said it would take my mind off unhealthy creatures like frogs and lizards and buffaloes. Once, when Toto tore the drawing room curtains, she put a needle and thread in my hand and made me stitch the curtain together, even though I made long, two-inch stitches which had to be taken out by Grandmother and done all over again.

She took the photograph from my hand and we both stared at it for quite some time. The girl had long, loose hair, and she wore a long dress that nearly covered her ankles and sleeves that reached her wrists; but, in spite of all this drapery, the girl appeared to be full of freedom and movement; she stood with her legs apart and her hands on her hips, and she had a wide, almost devilish smile on her face.

'Whose picture is it?' I asked.

'A little girl's, of course,' said Grandmother. 'Can't you tell?'

'Yes, but did you know her?'

'Oh yes, I knew her,' said Grandmother. 'But she was a wicked little girl, and I shouldn't tell you about her. I'll tell you about the photograph. It was taken in our home, oh many many years ago, and that's the garden wall, and over the wall there was a road leading to town. That girl used to sneak over the wall sometimes, and visit the bazaar. She couldn't resist jalebis. Do you like jalebis?'

'Yes, very much! But whose hands are they?' I asked,

'Coming up from the other side?'

Grandmother squinted and looked closely at the picture, shaking her head. 'It's the first time I've noticed,' she said, 'They must have been a child's, another child's.'

'Were they Grandfather's? Didn't he climb over the wall, afterwards?'

'No, nobody climbed up. At least, I don't remember.'

'And you remember well, Granny.'

'Yes, I remember... I remember what is not in the photograph. It was a spring day and there was a cool breeze blowing. Those flowers at the girl's feet, they were marigolds, and the bougainvillaea creeper was a mass of purple. You can't see those colours in the photo, and even if you could, wouldn't be able to smell the flowers or feel the breeze.'

'And what about the girl?' I asked. 'Tell me about the girl.'

'Well, she was a wicked girl,' said Grandmother. 'You don't know the trouble her mother had getting her into those fine clothes she's wearing.'

'They're terrible clothes,' I said.

'She thought so, too. Most of the time she hardly wore a thing. Dehradun summers were as hot then as they are now. She used to go swimming in the canal. The neighbours were shocked. Boys never teased her, because she didn't hesitate to fight them!'

'She looks tough,' I said.' 'You can tell by the way she's smiling. At any moment something's going to happen.'

'Something did happen,' said Grandmother. 'Her mother wouldn't let her get out of those awful clothes, so she jumped into the canal fully clothed!'

I burst into laughter and Grandmother joined in.

'Who was the girl?' I asked. 'You must tell me who she was.'

'No, that wouldn't do,' said Grandmother. 'I won't tell you.'

I knew the girl in the photograph was really Grandmother, I pretended not to know. I knew, because Grandmother still smiled in the same way.

'Come on, Granny,' I said. 'Tell me, tell me.'

But Grandmother shook her head and carried on with her knitting; and I held the photograph in my hands, looking from it to my grandmother and back again, trying to find points in common between the old lady and the little pigtailed girl. A butterfly settled on the end of Grandmother's knitting needle, and stayed there while the needle clicked away. I made a grab at the butterfly, and it flew off in a dipping flight and settled on a sunflower.

'I wonder whose hands they were,' whispered Grandmother to herself, with her head bowed in memory, and her needles clicking away in the soft, warm silence of that summer afternoon.

All this was many years ago.

When my parents returned to India, I left my grandparents' house and went to live in Saurashtra. Grandfather and I corresponded regularly and he kept me informed of his pets and any new additions to his zoo.

I often think about his birds and animals, the inhabitants of the banyan tree, and the residents of the pond behind the old house. And I remember Ramu the village boy, and the fun we had with the buffaloes. And I wish that I might see them again.

And perhaps one day when I have made some money I will go back to Dehradun and buy back Grandfather's old house and start another zoo of my own.

UNCLE KEN'S RUMBLE IN THE JUNGLE

Uncle Ken drove Grandfather's old Fiat along the Forest road at an incredible 30 mph scattering pheasants, partridges and jungle fowl as he scattered along. He had come in search of the disappearing Red Jungle Fowl, and I could see why the bird had disappeared. Too many noisy human beings had invaded its habitat.

By the time we reached the forest rest house, one of the car doors had fallen off its hinges, and a large lantana bush had got entwined in the bumper.

'Never mind,' said Uncle Ken. 'It's all part of the adventure.'

The rest house had been reserved for Uncle Ken, thanks to grandfather's good relations with the forest department. But I was the only other person in the car. No one else would trust himself or herself to Uncle Ken's driving. He treated a car as though it were a low-flying aircraft having some difficulty in getting of the runway.

As we arrived at the rest house, a number of hens made a dash for safety.

'Look, jungle fowl!' exclaimed Uncle Ken.

'Domestic fowl,' I said, 'They must belong to the forest guards.'

I was right, of course. One of the hens was destined to be served up as chicken curry later that day. The jungle birds avoided the neighbourhood of the rest house, just in case they were mistaken for poultry and went into the cooking-pot.

Uncle Ken was all for starting his search right away, and after a brief interval during which we were served with tea and pakoras (prepared by the forest guard, who it turned out was also a good cook), we set off on foot into the jungle in search of the elusive Red Jungle Fowl.

'No tigers around here! Are there?' asked Uncle Ken, just to be on the safe side.

'No tigers on this range,' said the guard, 'Just elephants.'

Uncle Ken wasn't afraid of elephants. He'd been for numerous elephants rides at the Lucknow zoo. He'd also seen Sabu in 'Elephant Boy'.

A small wooden bridge took us across a little river, and then we were in third jungle, following the forest guard who led us along a path that was frequently blocked by broken tree branches and pieces of bamboo.

'Why all these broken branches?' asked Uncle Ken.

'The elephants sir,' replied our guard, 'They passed through last night. They like certain leaves, as well as young bamboo shoots.'

We saw a number of spotted deer and several pheasants, but no Red jungle fowl.

That evening we sat out on the veranda of the rest house.

All was silent except for the distant trumpeting of elephants. Then, from the stream, came the chanting of hundreds of frogs.

There were tenors and baritones, sopranos and contraltos, and occasionally a bass deep enough to have pleased the great Chaliapin. They sang duets and quartets from *La Boheme* and other Italian operas, drowsing out all other jungle sounds except for the occasional cry of a jackal doing his best to join in.

'We might as well sing too,' said Uncle Ken, and began singing the 'Indian Love Call' in his best Nelson Eddy manner.

The frogs fell silent, obviously awestruck; but instead of receiving an answering love-call, Uncle Ken was answered by even more strident jackal calls—not one, but several—with the result that all self-respecting denizens of the forest fled from the vicinity, and we saw no wildlife that night apart from a frightened rabbit that sped across the clearing and vanished into the darkness.

Early next morning we renewed our efforts to track down the Red Jungle Fowl, but it remained elusive. Returning to the rest house dusty and weary, Uncle Ken exclaimed: 'There it is—a Red Jungle Fowl!'

But it turned out to be the caretaker's cock-bird, a handsome fellow all red and gold, but not the jungle variety.

Disappointed, Uncle Ken decided to return to civilization. Another night in the rest house did not appeal to him. He had run out of songs to sing.

In any case, the weather had changed overnight and a light drizzle was falling as we started out. This had turned to a steady downpour by the time we reached the bridge across the Suseva River. And standing in the middle of the bridge was an elephant.

He was a long tusker and he didn't look too friendly.

Uncle Ken blew his horn, and that was a mistake.

It was a strident, penetrating horn, highly effective on city roads but out of place in the forest.

The elephant took it as a challenge, and returned the blast of the horn with a shrill trumpeting of its own. It took a few steps forward. Uncle Ken put the car into reverse.

'Is there another way out of here?' he asked.

'There's a side road,' I said, recalling an earlier trip with grandfather, 'It will take us to the Kansrao railway station.'

'What ho!' cried Uncle Ken. 'To the station we go!'

And he turned the car and drove back until we came to the turning.

The narrow road was now a rushing torrent of rain water and all Uncle Ken's driving-skills were put to the test. He had on one occasion driven through a brick wall, so he knew all about obstacles; but they were usually stationary ones.

'More elephants,' I said, as two large pachyderms loomed out of the rain-drenched forest.

'Elephants to the right of us, elephants to the left of us!' chanted Uncle Ken, misquoting Tennyson's 'Charge of the Light Brigade,' 'Into the valley of death rode the six hundred!'

'There are now three of them,' I observed.

'Not my lucky number,' said Uncle Ken and pressed hard on the accelerator. We lurched forward, almost running over a terrified barking-deer.

'Is four your lucky number, Uncle Ken?'

'Why do you ask?'

'Well, there are now four of them behind us. And they are

catching up quite fast!'

'I see the station ahead,' cried Uncle Ken, as we drove into a clearing where a tiny railway station stood like a beacon of safety in the wilderness.

The car came to a grinding halt. We abandoned it and ran for the building.

The station-master saw our predicament, and beckoned to us to enter the station building, which was little more than a two-room shed and platform. He took us inside his tiny control room and shut the steel gate behind us.

'The elephants won't bother you here,' he said. 'But say goodbye to your car.'

We looked out of the window and were horrified to see Grandfather's Fiat overturned by one of the elephants, while another proceeded to trample it underfoot. The other elephants joined in the mayhem and soon the car was a flattened piece of junk.

'I'm station-master Abdul Ranf,' the station-master introduced himself. 'I know a good scrap-dealer in Doiwala. I'll give you his address.'

'But how do we get out of here?' asked Uncle Ken.

'Well, it's only an hour's walk to Doiwala, not with those elephants around. Stay and have a cup of tea. The Dehra Express will pass through shortly. It stops for a few minutes. And it's only half-an-hour to Dehra from here.' He punched out a couple of rail tickets, 'Here you are, my friends. Just two rupees each. The cheapest rail journey in India. And these tickets carry an insurance value of two lakh rupees each, should an accident befall you between here and Dehradun.'

Uncle Ken's eyes lit up.

'You mean, if one of us falls out of the train?' he asked.

'Out of the moving train,' clarified the station-master. 'There will be an enquiry, of course, some people try to fake an accident.'

But Uncle Ken decided against falling out of the train and making a fortune. He'd had enough excitement for the day. We got home safely enough, taking a pony-cart from Dehradun station to our house.

'Where's my car?' asked Grandfather, as we staggered up the veranda steps.

'It had a small accident,' said Uncle Ken. 'We left it outside the Kansrao railway station. I'll collect it later.'

'I'm starving,' I said. 'Haven't eaten since morning.'

'Well, come and have your dinner,' said Granny. 'I've made something special for you. One of your grandfather's hunting friends sent us a jungle fowl. I've made a nice roast. Try it with apple sauce.'

Uncle Ken did not ask if the jungle fowl was red, grey or technicoloured. He was first to the dining table.

Granny had anticipated this, and served me with a chicken leg, giving the other leg to grandfather.

'I rather fancy the breast myself,' she said, and this left Uncle Ken with a long and scrawny neck—which was more than he deserved.

A CROW FOR ALL SEASONS

Early to bed and early to rise makes a crow healthy, wealthy and wise.

They say it's true for humans too. I'm not so sure about that. But for crows it's a must.

I'm always up at the crack of dawn, often the first crow to break the night's silence with a lusty caw. My friends and relatives, who roost in the same tree, grumble a bit and mutter to themselves, but they are soon cawing just as loudly. Long before the sun is up, we set off on the day's work.

We do not pause even for the morning wash. Later in the day, if it's hot and muggy, I might take a dip in some human's bath water; but early in the morning we like to be up and about before everyone else. This is the time when trash cans and refuse dumps are overflowing with goodies, and we like to sift through them before the dustmen arrive in their disposal trucks.

Not that we are afraid of a famine in refuse. As human beings multiply, so does their rubbish.

Only yesterday I rescued an old typewriter ribbon from the dustbin, just before it was emptied. What a waste that would have been! I had no use for it myself, but I gave it to one of my cousins who got married recently, and she tells me it's just right for her nest, the one she's building on a telegraph pole. It helps her bind the twigs together, she says.

My own preference is for toothbrushes. They're just a hobby really, like stamp-collecting with humans. I have a small but select collection which I keep in a hole in the garden wall. Don't ask me how many I've got—crows don't believe there's any point in counting beyond two—but I know there's more than *one*, that there's a whole lot of them in fact, because there isn't anyone living on this road who hasn't lost a toothbrush to me at some time or another.

We crows living in the jackfruit tree have this stretch of road to ourselves, but so that we don't quarrel or have misunderstandings we've shared the houses out. I picked the bungalow with the orchard at the back. After all, I don't eat rubbish and throwaways all the time. Just occasionally, I like a ripe guava or the soft flesh of a papaya. And sometimes I like the odd beetle as an *hors d'oeuvre*. Those humans in the bungalow should be grateful to me for keeping down the population of fruit-eating beetles, and even for recycling their refuse; but no, humans are never grateful. No sooner do I settle in one of their guava trees than stones are whizzing past me. So I return to the dustbin on the back veranda steps. They don't mind my being there.

One of my cousins shares the bungalow with me, but he's a lazy fellow and I have to do most of the foraging. Sometimes I get him to lend me a claw, but most of the time he's preening his feathers and trying to look handsome for a pretty young thing who lives in the banyan tree at the next turning.

When he's in the mood he can be invaluable, as he proved recently when I was having some difficulty getting at the dog's food on the veranda.

This dog, who is fussed over so much by the humans, I've adopted is a great big fellow, a mastiff who pretends to a pedigree going back to the time of Genghis Khan—he likes to pretend one of his ancestors was the great Khan's watchdog. But, as often happens in famous families, animal or human, there is a falling off in quality over a period of time, and this huge fellow—Tiger, they call him—is a case in point. All brawn and no brain. Many's the time I've removed a juicy bone from his plate or helped myself to pickings from under his nose.

But of late he's been growing canny and selfish. He doesn't like to share any more. And the other day I was almost in his jaws when he took a sudden lunge at me. Snap went his great teeth; but all he got was one of my tail feathers. He spat it out in disgust. Who wants crow's meat, anyway?

All the same, I thought, I'd better not be too careless. It's not for nothing that a crow's IQ is way above that of all other birds. And it's higher than a dog's, I bet.

I woke Cousin Slow from his midday siesta and said, 'Hey, Slow, we've got a problem. If you want any of that delicious tripe today, you've got to lend a claw—or a beak. That dog's getting snappier day by day.'

Slow opened one eye and said, 'Well, if you insist. But you know how I hate getting into a scuffle. It's bad for the gloss on my feathers.'

'I don't insist,' I said politely. 'But I'm not foraging for both of us today. It's every crow for himself.'

'Okay, okay, I'm coming,' said Slow, and with barely a flap he dropped down from the tree to the wall.

'What's the strategy?' I asked.

'Simple. We'll just give him the old one-two.'

We flew across to the veranda. Tiger had just started his meal. He was a fast, greedy eater who made horrible slurping sounds while he guzzled his food. We had to move fast if we wanted to get something before the meal was over.

I sidled up to Tiger and wished him good afternoon.

He kept on gobbling—but quicker now.

Slow came up from behind and gave him a quick peck near the tail—a sensitive spot—and, as Tiger swung round, snarling, I moved in quickly and snatched up several tidbits.

Tiger went for me, and I flew freestyle for the garden wall. The dish was untended, so Slow helped himself to as many scraps as he could stuff in his mouth.

He joined me on the garden wall, and we sat there feasting, while Tiger barked himself hoarse below.

'Go catch a cat,' said Slow, who is given to slang. 'You're in the wrong league, big boy.'

The great sage Pratyasataka—ever heard of him? I guess not—once said, 'Nothing can improve a crow.'

Like most human sages he wasn't very clear in his thinking, so that there has been some misunderstanding about what he meant. Humans like to think that what he really meant was that crows were so bad as to be beyond improvement. But we crows know better. We interpret the saying as meaning that the crow is so perfect that no improvement is possible.

It's not that we aren't human—what I mean is, there are times when we fall from our high standards and do rather foolish things. Like at lunchtime the other day.

Sometimes, when the table is laid in the bungalow, and before the family enters the dining room, I nip in through the open window and make a quick foray among the dishes. Sometimes I'm lucky enough to pick up a sausage or a slice of toast, or even a pat of butter, making off before someone enters and throws a bread knife at me. But on this occasion, just as I was reaching for the toast, a thin slouching fellow—Junior Sahib they call him—entered suddenly and shouted at me. I was so startled that I leapt across the table seeking shelter. Something flew at me, and in an effort to dodge the missile, I put my head through a circular object and then found it wouldn't come off.

It wasn't safe to hang around there, so I flew out the window with this dashed ring still round my neck.

Serviette or napkin rings, that's what they are called. Quite unnecessary objects, but some humans—particularly the well-to-do sort—seem to like having them on their tables, holding bits of cloth in place. The cloth is used for wiping the mouth. Have you ever heard of such nonsense?

Anyway, there I was with a fat napkin ring round my neck, and as I perched on the wall trying to get it off, the entire human family gathered on their veranda to watch me.

There was the Colonel Sahib and his wife, the Memsahib; there was the scrawny Junior Sahib (worst of the lot); there was a mischievous boy (the Colonel Sahib's grandson) known as the Baba; there was the cook (who usually flung orange peels at me) and the gardener (who once tried to decapitate me with a spade), and the dog Tiger who, like most dogs, tries unsuccessfully to be human.

Today they weren't cursing and shaking their fists at me; they were just standing and laughing their heads off. What's so funny about a crow with its head stuck in a napkin ring?

Worse was to follow.

The noise had attracted the other crows in the area, and if there's one thing crows detest, it's a crow who doesn't look like a crow.

They swooped low and dived on me, hammering at the wretched napkin ring, until they had knocked me off the wall and into a flower bed. Then six or seven toughs landed on me with every intention of finishing me off.

'Hey, boys!' I cawed. 'This is me, Speedy! What are you trying to do—kill me?'

'That's right! You don't look like Speedy to us. What have you done with him, eh?'

And they set upon me with even greater vigour.

'You're just like a bunch of lousy humans!' I shouted. 'You're no better than them—this is just the way they carry on amongst themselves!'

That brought them to a halt. They stopped trying to peck me to pieces, and stood back, looking puzzled. The napkin ring had been shattered in the onslaught and had fallen to the ground.

'Why, it's Speedy!' said one of the gang.

'None other!'

'Good old Speedy—what are you doing here? And where's the guy we were hammering just now?'

There was no point in trying to explain things to them.

Crows are like that. They're all good pals—until one of them tries to look different. Then he could be just another bird.

'He took off for Tibet,' I said. 'It was getting unhealthy for him around here.'

◆

Summertime is here again. And although I'm a crow for all seasons, I must admit to a preference for the summer months.

Humans grow lazy and don't pursue me with so much vigour. Garbage cans overflow. Food goes bad and is constantly being thrown away. Overripe fruit gets tastier by the minute. If fellows like me weren't around to mop up all these unappreciated riches, how would humans manage?

There's one character in the bungalow, Junior Sahib, who will never appreciate our services, it seems. He simply hates crows. The small boy may throw stones at us occasionally, but then, he's the sort who throws stones at almost anything. There's nothing personal about it. He just throws stones on principle.

The Memsahib is probably the best of the lot. She often throws me scraps from the kitchen—onion skins, potato peels, crusts and leftovers—and even when I nip in and make off with something not meant for me (like a jam tart or a cheese pakora) she is quite sporting about it. The Junior Sahib looks outraged, but the lady of the house says, 'Well, we've all got to make a living somehow, and that's how crows make theirs. It's high time you thought of earning a living.' Junior Sahib's her nephew—that's his occupation. He has never been known to work.

The Colonel Sahib has a sense of humour but it's often directed at me. He thinks I'm a comedian.

He discovered I'd been making off with the occasional egg from the egg basket on the veranda, and one day, without my knowledge, he made a substitution.

Right on top of the pile I found a smooth round egg, and before anyone could shout, 'Crow!' I'd made off with it. It was abnormally light. I put it down on the lawn and set about cracking it with my strong beak, but it would keep slipping away or bounding off into the bushes. Finally, I got it between my feet and gave it a good hard whack. It burst open, and to my utter astonishment, there was nothing inside!

I looked up and saw the old man standing on the veranda, doubled up with laughter.

'What are you laughing at?' asked the Memsahib, coming out to see what it was all about.

'It's that ridiculous crow!' guffawed the Colonel, pointing at me. 'You know he's been stealing our eggs. Well, I placed a ping pong ball on top of the pile, and he fell for it! He's been struggling with that ball for twenty minutes! That will teach him a lesson.'

It did. But I had my revenge later, when I pinched a brand new toothbrush from the Colonel's bathroom.

The Junior Sahib has no sense of humour at all. He idles about the house and grounds all day, whistling or singing to himself.

'Even that crow sings better than Uncle,' said the boy.

A truthful boy; but all he got for his honesty was a whack on the head from his uncle.

Anyway, as a gesture of appreciation, I perched on the garden wall and gave the family a rendering of my favourite crow song, which is my own composition. Here it is, translated for your benefit:

> Oh, for the life of a crow!
> A bird who's in the know.
> Although we are cursed,
> We are never dispersed—
> We're always on the go!
> I know I'm a bit of a rogue
> (And my voice wouldn't pass for a brogue),
> But there's no one as sleek
> Or as neat with his beak—
> So they're putting my picture in Vogue!
> Oh, for the life of a crow!
> I reap what I never sow,
> They call me a thief,
> Pray I'll soon come to grief—
> But there's no getting rid of a crow!

I gave it everything I had, and the humans—all of them on the lawn to enjoy the evening breeze, listened to me in silence, struck with wonder at my performance.

When I had finished, I bowed and preened myself, waiting for the applause.

They stared at each other for a few seconds. Then the Junior Sahib stooped, picked up a bottle opener, and flung it at me.

Well, I ask you!

What can one say about humans? I do my best to defend them from all kinds of criticism, and this is what I get for my pains.

Anyway, I picked up the bottle opener and added it to my collection of odds and ends.

It was getting dark, and soon everyone was stumbling around, looking for another bottle opener. Junior Sahib's popularity was even lower than mine.

One day, Junior Sahib came home carrying a heavy shotgun. He pointed it at me a few times and I dived for cover. But he didn't fire. Probably I was out of range.

'He's only threatening you,' said Slow from the safety of the jamun tree, where he sat in the shadows. 'He probably doesn't know how to fire the thing.'

But I wasn't taking any chances. I'd seen a sly look on Junior Sahib's face, and I decided that he was trying to make me careless. So I stayed well out of range.

Then one evening, I received a visit from my cousin, Charm. He'd come to me for a loan. He wanted some new bottle tops for his collection and had brought me a mouldy old toothbrush to offer in exchange.

Charm landed on the garden wall, toothbrush in his break, and was waiting for me to join him there, when there was a flash and a tremendous bang. Charm was sent several feet into the air, and landed limp and dead in a flower bed.

'I've got him, I've got him!' shouted Junior Sahib. 'I've shot that blasted crow!'

Throwing away the gun, Junior Sahib ran out into the garden, overcome with joy. He picked up my fallen relative, and began running around the bungalow with his trophy.

The rest of the family had collected on the veranda.

'Drop that thing at once!' called the Memsahib.

'Uncle is doing a war dance,' observed the boy.

'It's unlucky to shoot a crow,' said the Colonel.

I thought it was time to take a hand in the proceedings and let everyone know that the right crow—the one and only Speedy—was alive and kicking. So I swooped down the jackfruit tree, dived through Junior Sahib's window, and emerged with one of his socks.

Triumphantly flaunting his dead crow, Junior Sahib came dancing up the garden path, then stopped dead when he saw me perched on the window sill, a sock in my beak. His jaw fell, his eyes bulged; he looked like the owl in the banyan tree.

'You shot the wrong crow!' shouted the Colonel, and everyone roared with laughter.

Before Junior Sahib could recover from the shock, I took off in a leisurely fashion and joined Slow on the wall.

Junior Sahib came rushing out with the gun, but by now it was too dark to see anything, and I heard the Memsahib telling the Colonel, 'You'd better take that gun away before he does himself a mischief.' So the Colonel took Junior Sahib indoors and gave him a brandy.

I composed a new song for Junior Sahib's benefit, and sang it to him outside his window early next morning:

I understand you want a crow
To poison, shoot or smother;
My fond salaams, but by your leave
I'll substitute another;
Allow me then, to introduce
My most respected brother.

Although I was quite understanding about the whole tragic mix-up—I was, after all, the family's very own house crow—my fellow crows were outraged at what had happened to Charm, and swore vengeance on Junior Sahib.

'*Corvus splendens!*' they shouted with great spirit, forgetting that this title had been bestowed on us by a human. In times of war, we forget how much we owe to our enemies.

Junior Sahib had only to step into the garden, and several crows would swoop down on him, screeching and swearing and aiming lusty blows at his head and hands. He took to coming out wearing a sola topi, and even then they knocked it off and drove him indoors. Once he tried lighting a cigarette on the veranda steps, when Slow swooped low across the porch and snatched it from his lips.

Junior Sahib shut himself up in his room, and smoked countless cigarettes—a sure sign that his nerves were going to pieces.

Every now and then, the Memsahib would come out and shoo us off; and because she wasn't an enemy, we obliged by retreating to the garden wall. After all, Slow and I depended on her for much of our board if not for our lodging. But Junior Sahib had only to show his face outside the house, and all the crows in the area would be after him like avenging furies.

'It doesn't look as though they are going to forgive you,' said the Memsahib.

'Elephants never forget, and crows never forgive,' said the Colonel.

'Would you like to borrow my catapult, Uncle?' asked the boy. 'Just for self-protection, you know.'

'Shut up,' said Junior Sahib and went to bed.

One day, he sneaked out of the back door and dashed across to the garage. A little later the family's old car, seldom used, came out of the garage with Junior Sahib at the wheel. He'd decided that if he couldn't take a walk in safety he'd go for a drive. All the windows were up.

No sooner had the car turned into the driveway than about a dozen crows dived down on it, crowding the bonnet and flapping in front of the windscreen. Junior Sahib couldn't see a thing. He swung the steering wheel left, right and centre, and the car went off the driveway, ripped through a hedge, crushed a bed of sweetpeas and came to a stop against the trunk of a mango tree.

Junior Sahib just sat there, afraid to open the door. The family had to come out of the house and rescue him.

'Are you all right?' asked the Colonel.

'I've bruised my knees,' said Junior Sahib.

'Never mind your knees,' said the Memsahib, gazing around at the ruin of her garden. 'What about my sweetpeas?'

'I think your uncle is going to have a nervous breakdown,' I heard the Colonel saying to the boy.

'What's that?' asked the boy. 'Is it the same as a car having a breakdown?'

'Well, not exactly... But you could call it a mind breaking down.'

Junior Sahib had been refusing to leave his room or take his meals. The family was worried about him. I was worried, too. Believe it or not, we crows are among the very few birds who sincerely desire the preservation of the human species.

'He needs a change,' said the Memsahib.

'A rest cure,' said the Colonel sarcastically. 'A rest from doing nothing.'

'Send him to Switzerland,' suggested the boy.

'We can't afford that. But we can take him up to a hill station.'

The nearest hill station was some fifty miles as the human drives (only ten as the crow flies). Many people went up there during the summer months. It wasn't fancied much by crows. For one thing, it was a tidy sort of place, and people lived in houses that were set fairly far apart. Opportunities for scavenging were limited. Also it was rather cold and the trees were inconvenient and uncomfortable. A friend of mine, who had spent a night in a pine tree, said he hadn't been able to sleep because of the prickly pine needles and the wind howling through the branches.

'Let's all go up for a holiday,' said the Memsahib. 'We can spend a week in a boarding house. All of us need a change.'

A few days later the house was locked up, and the family piled into the old car and drove off to the hills.

I had the grounds to myself.

The dog had gone too, and the gardener spent all day dozing in his hammock. There was no one around to trouble me.

'We've got the whole place to ourselves,' I told Slow.

'Yes, but what good is that? With everyone gone, there are no throwaways, giveaways and takeaways!'

'We'll have to try the house next door.'

'And be driven off by the other crows? That's not our territory, you know. We can go across to help them, or to ask for their help, but we're not supposed to take their pickings. It just isn't cricket, old boy.'

We could have tried the bazaar or the railway station, where there is always a lot of rubbish to be found, but there is also a lot of competition in those places. The station crows are gangsters. The bazaar crows are bullies. Slow and I had grown soft. We'd have been no match for the bad boys.

'I've just realized how much we depend on humans,' I said.

'We could go back to living in the jungle,' said Slow.

'No, that would be too much like hard work. We'd be living on wild fruit most of the time. Besides, the jungle crows won't have anything to do with us now. Ever since we took up with humans, we became the outcasts of the bird world.'

'That means we're almost human.'

'You might say we have all their vices and none of their virtues.'

'Just a different set of values, old boy.'

'Like eating hens' eggs instead of crows' eggs. That's something in their favour. And while you're hanging around here waiting for the mangoes to fall, I'm off to locate our humans.'

Slow's beak fell open. He looked like—well, a hungry crow.

'Don't tell me you're going to follow them up to the hill station? You don't even know where they are staying.'

'I'll soon find out,' I said, and took off for the hills.

You'd be surprised at how simple it is to be a good detective, if only you put your mind to it. Of course, if Ellery Queen had been able to fly, he wouldn't have required fifteen chapters and his father's assistance to crack a case.

Swooping low over the hill station, it wasn't long before I spotted my humans' old car. It was parked outside a boarding house called Climber's Rest. I hadn't seen anyone climbing, but dozing in an armchair in the garden was my favourite human.

I perched on top of a colourful umbrella and waited for Junior Sahib to wake up. I decided it would be rather inconsiderate of me to disturb his sleep, so I waited patiently on the brolly, looking at him with one eye and keeping one eye on the house. He stirred uneasily, as though he'd suddenly had a bad dream; then he opened his eyes. I must have been the first thing he saw.

'Good morning,' I cawed in a friendly tone—always ready to forgive and forget, that's Speedy!

He leapt out of the armchair and ran into the house, hollering at the top of his voice.

I supposed he hadn't been able to contain his delight at seeing me again. Humans can be funny that way. They'll hate you one day and love you the next.

Well, Junior Sahib ran all over the boarding house screaming: 'It's that crow, it's that crow! He's following me everywhere!'

Various people, including the family, ran outside to see what the commotion was about, and I thought it would be better to make myself scarce. So I flew to the top of a spruce tree and stayed very still and quiet.

'Crow! What crow?' said the Colonel.

'Our crow!' cried Junior Sahib. 'The one that persecutes me. I was dreaming of it just now, and when I opened my eyes, there it was, on the garden umbrella!'

'There's nothing there now,' said the Memsahib. 'You probably hadn't woken up completely.'

'He is having illusions again,' said the boy.

'Delusions,' corrected the Colonel.

'Now look here,' said the Memsahib, 'you'll have to pull yourself together. You'll take leave of your senses if you don't.'

'I tell you, it's here!' sobbed Junior Sahib. 'It's following me everywhere.'

'It's grown fond of Uncle,' said the boy. 'And it seems Uncle can't live without crows.'

Junior Sahib looked up with a wild glint in his eye.

'That's it!' he cried. 'I can't live without them. That's the answer to my problem. I don't hate crows—I love them!'

Everyone just stood around goggling at Junior Sahib.

'I'm feeling fine now,' he carried on. 'What a difference it makes if you can just do the opposite of what you've been doing before! I thought I hated crows. But all the time I really loved them!' And flapping his arms, and trying to caw like a crow, he went prancing about the garden.

'Now he thinks he's a crow,' said the boy. 'Is he still having delusions?'

'That's right,' said the Memsahib. 'Delusions of grandeur.'

After that, the family decided that there was no point in staying on in the hill station any longer. Junior Sahib had completed his rest cure. And even if he was the only one who believed himself cured, that was all right, because after all he was the one who mattered... If you're feeling fine, can there be anything wrong with you?

No sooner was everyone back in the bungalow than Junior Sahib took to hopping barefoot on the grass early every morning, all the time scattering food about for the crows. Bread, chappattis, cooked rice, curried eggplants, the Memsahib's homemade toffee—you name it, we got it!

Slow and I were the first to help ourselves to these dawn offerings, and soon the other crows had joined us on the lawn. We didn't mind. Junior Sahib brought enough for everyone.

'We ought to honour him in some way,' said Slow.

'Yes, why not?' said I. 'There was someone else, hundreds of years ago, who fed the birds. They followed him wherever he went.'

'That's right. They made him a saint. But as far as I know, he didn't feed any crows. At least, you don't see any crows in the pictures—just sparrows and robins and wagtails.'

'Small fry. Our human is dedicated exclusively to crows. Do you realize that, Slow?'

'Sure. We ought to make him the patron saint of crows. What do you say, fellows?'

'Caw, caw, caw!' All the crows were in agreement.

'St Corvus!' said Slow as Junior Sahib emerged from the house, laden with good things to eat.

'Corvus, corvus, corvus!' we cried.

And what a pretty picture he made—a crow eating from his hand, another perched on his shoulder, and about a dozen of us on the grass, forming a respectful ring around him.

From persecutor to protector; from beastliness to saintliness. And sometimes it can be the other way round: you never know with humans!

MONKEY TROUBLE

Grandfather bought Tutu from a street entertainer for the sum of ten rupees. The man had three monkeys. Tutu was the smallest, but the most mischievous. She was tied up most of the time. The little monkey looked so miserable with a collar and chain that Grandfather decided it would be much happier in our home. Grandfather had a weakness for keeping unusual pets. It was a habit that I, at the age of eight or nine, used to encourage.

Grandmother at first objected to having a monkey in the house. 'You have enough pets as it is,' she said, referring to Grandfather's goat, several white mice and a small tortoise.

'But I don't have any,' I said.

'You're wicked enough for two monkeys. One boy in the house is all I can take.'

'Ah, but Tutu isn't a boy,' said Grandfather triumphantly. 'This is a little girl monkey!'

Grandmother gave in. She had always wanted a little girl in the house. She believed girls were less troublesome than boys. Tutu was to prove her wrong.

She was a pretty little monkey. Her bright eyes sparkled with mischief beneath deep-set eyebrows. And her teeth, which were a pearly white, were often revealed in a grin that frightened the wits out of Aunt Ruby, whose nerves had already suffered from the presence of Grandfather's pet python. But this was my grandparents' house, and aunts and uncles had to put up with our pets.

Tutu's hands had a dried-up look, as though they had been pickled in the sun for many years. One of the first things I taught her was to shake hands, and this she insisted on doing with all who visited the house. Peppery Major Malik would have to stoop and shake hands with Tutu before he could enter the drawing room, otherwise Tutu would climb onto his shoulder and stay there, roughing up his hair and playing with his moustache.

Uncle Benji couldn't stand any of our pets and took a particular dislike to Tutu, who was always making faces at him. But as Uncle Benji was never in a job for long, and depended on Grandfather's good-natured generosity, he had to shake hands with Tutu, like everyone else.

Tutu's fingers were quick and wicked. And her tail, while adding to her good looks (Grandfather believed a tail would add to anyone's good looks!), also served as a third hand. She could use it to hang from a branch, and it was capable of scooping up any delicacy that might be out of reach of her hands.

On one of Aunt Ruby's visits, loud shrieks from her bedroom brought us running to see what was wrong. It was only Tutu trying on Aunt Ruby's petticoats! They were much too large, of course, and when Aunt Ruby entered the room, all she saw was a faceless white blob jumping up and down on the bed.

We disentangled Tutu and soothed Aunt Ruby. I gave Tutu a bunch of sweet peas to make her happy. Granny didn't like anyone plucking her sweet peas, so I took some from Major Malik's garden while he was having his afternoon siesta.

Then Uncle Benji complained that his hairbrush was missing. We found Tutu sunning herself on the back veranda, using the hairbrush to scratch her armpits.

I took it from her and handed it back to Uncle Benji with an apology; but he flung the brush away with an oath.

'Such a fuss about nothing,' I said. 'Tutu doesn't have fleas!'

'No, and she bathes more often than Benji,' said Grandfather, who had borrowed Aunt Ruby's shampoo to give Tutu a bath.

All the same, Grandmother objected to Tutu being given the run of the house. Tutu had to spend her nights in the outhouse, in the company of the goat. They got on quite well, and it was not long before Tutu was seen sitting comfortably on the back of the goat, while the goat roamed the back garden in search of its favourite grass.

The day Grandfather had to visit Meerut to collect his railway pension, he decided to take Tutu and me along to keep us both out of mischief, he said. To prevent Tutu from wandering about on the train, causing inconvenience to passengers, she was provided with a large black travelling bag. This, with some straw at the bottom, became her compartment. Grandfather and I paid for our seats, and we took Tutu along as hand baggage.

There was enough space for Tutu to look out of the bag occasionally, and to be fed with bananas and biscuits, but she could not get her hands through the opening and the canvas was too strong for her to bite her way through.

Tutu's efforts to get out only had the effect of making the bag roll about on the floor or occasionally jump into the air—an exhibition that attracted a curious crowd of onlookers at the Dehra and Meerut railway stations.

Anyway, Tutu remained in the bag as far as Meerut, but while Grandfather was producing our tickets at the turnstile, she suddenly poked her head out of the bag and gave the ticket collector a wide grin.

The poor man was taken aback. But, with great presence of mind and much to Grandfather's annoyance, he said, 'Sir, you have a dog with you. You'll have to buy a ticket for it.'

'It's not a dog!' said Grandfather indignantly. 'This is a baby monkey of the species *macacus mischievous*, closely related to the human species *homus horriblis*! And there is no charge for babies!'

'It's as big as a cat,' said the ticket collector. 'Cats and dogs have to be paid for.'

'But, I tell you, it's only a baby!' protested Grandfather.

'Have you a birth certificate to prove that?' demanded the ticket collector.

'Next, you'll be asking to see her mother,' snapped Grandfather.

In vain did he take Tutu out of the bag. In vain did he try to prove that a young monkey did not qualify as a dog or a cat or even as a quadruped. Tutu was classified as a dog by the ticket collector, and five rupees were handed over as her fare.

Then Grandfather, just to get his own back, took from his pocket the small tortoise that he sometimes carried about, and said: 'And what must I pay for this, since you charge for all creatures great and small?'

The ticket collector looked closely at the tortoise, prodded it with his forefinger, gave Grandfather a triumphant look, and said, 'No charge, sir. It is not a dog!'

◆

Winters in North India can be very cold. A great treat for Tutu on winter evenings was the large bowl of hot water given to her by Grandfather for a bath. Tutu would cunningly test the temperature with her hand, then gradually step into the bath, first one foot, then the other (as she had seen me doing) until she was in the water upto her neck.

Once comfortable, she would take the soap in her hands or feet and rub herself all over. When the water became cold, she would get out and run as quickly as she could to the kitchen fire in order to dry herself. If anyone laughed at her during this performance, Tutu's feelings would be hurt and she would refuse to go on with the bath.

One day Tutu almost succeeded in boiling herself alive. Grandmother had left a large kettle on the fire for tea. And Tutu, all by herself and with nothing better to do, decided to remove the lid. Finding the water just warm enough for a bath, she got in, with her head sticking out from the open kettle.

This was fine for a while, until the water began to get heated. Tutu raised herself a little. But finding it cold outside, she sat down again. She continued hopping up and down for some time, until Grandmother returned and hauled her, half-boiled, out of the kettle.

'What's for tea today?' asked Uncle Benji gleefully. 'Boiled eggs and a half-boiled monkey?'

But Tutu was none the worse for the adventure and continued to bathe more regularly than Uncle Benji.

Aunt Ruby was a frequent taker of baths. This met with Tutu's approval—so much so that, one day, when Aunt Ruby had finished shampooing her hair, she looked up through a lather of bubbles and soap suds to see Tutu sitting opposite her in the bath, following her example.

◆

One day Aunt Ruby took us all by surprise. She announced that she had become engaged. We had always thought Aunt Ruby would never marry—she had often said so herself—but it appeared that the right man had now come along in the person of Rocky Fernandes, a schoolteacher from Goa.

Rocky was a tall, firm-jawed, good-natured man, a couple of years younger than Aunt Ruby. He had a fine baritone voice and sang in the manner of the great Nelson Eddy. As Grandmother liked baritone singers, Rocky was soon in her good books.

'But what on earth does he see in her?' Uncle Benji wanted to know.

'More than any girl has seen in you!' snapped Grandmother. 'Ruby's a fine girl. And they're both teachers. Maybe they can start a school of their own.'

Rocky visited the house quite often and brought me chocolates and cashew nuts, of which he seemed to have an unlimited supply. He also taught me several marching songs. Naturally, I approved of Rocky. Aunt Ruby won my grudging admiration for having made such a wise choice.

One day I overheard them talking of going to the bazaar to buy an engagement ring. I decided I would go along, too. But as Aunt Ruby had made it clear that she did not want me around, I decided that I had better follow at a discreet distance. Tutu, becoming aware that a mission of some importance was under way, decided to follow me. But as I had not invited her along, she too decided to keep out of sight.

Once in the crowded bazaar, I was able to get quite close to Aunt Ruby and Rocky without being spotted. I waited until they had settled down in a large jewellery shop before sauntering past and spotting them, as though by accident. Aunt Ruby wasn't too pleased at seeing me, but Rocky waved and called out, 'Come and join us! Help your aunt choose a beautiful ring!'

The whole thing seemed to be a waste of good money, but I did not say so—Aunt Ruby was giving me one of her more unloving looks.

'Look, these are pretty!' I said, pointing to some cheap, bright agates set in white metal. But Aunt Ruby wasn't looking. She was immersed in a case of diamonds.

'Why not a ruby for Aunt Ruby?' I suggested, trying to please her.

'That's her lucky stone,' said Rocky. 'Diamonds are the thing for engagements.' And he started singing a song about a diamond being a girl's best friend.

While the jeweller and Aunt Ruby were sifting through the diamond rings, and Rocky was trying out another tune, Tutu had slipped into the shop without being noticed by anyone but me. A little squeal of delight was the first sign she gave of her presence. Everyone looked up to see her trying on a pretty necklace.

'And what are those stones?' I asked.

'They look like pearls,' said Rocky.

'They *are* pearls,' said the shopkeeper, making a grab for them.

'It's that dreadful monkey!' cried Aunt Ruby. 'I knew that boy would bring her here!'

The necklace was already adorning Tutu's neck. I thought she looked rather nice in pearls, but she gave us no time to admire the effect. Springing out of our reach, Tutu dodged around Rocky, slipped between my legs, and made for the crowded road. I ran after her, shouting to her to stop, but she wasn't listening.

There were no branches to assist Tutu in her progress, but she used the heads and shoulders of people as springboards and so made rapid headway through the bazaar.

The jeweller left his shop and ran after us. So did Rocky. So did several bystanders who had seen the incident. And others, who had no idea what it was all about, joined in the chase. As Grandfather used to say, 'In a crowd, everyone plays follow-the-leader, even when they don't know who's leading.' Not everyone knew that the leader was Tutu. Only the front runners could see her.

She tried to make her escape speedier by leaping onto the back of a passing scooterist. The scooter swerved into a fruit stall and came to a standstill under a heap of bananas, while the scooterist found himself in the arms of an indignant fruitseller. Tutu peeled a banana and ate part of it, before deciding to move on.

From an awning, she made an emergency landing on a washerman's donkey. The donkey promptly panicked and rushed down the road, while bundles of washing fell by the wayside. The washerman joined in the chase. Children on their way to school decided that there was something better to do than attend classes. With shouts of glee, they soon overtook their panting elders.

Tutu finally left the bazaar and took a road leading in the direction of our house. But knowing that she would be caught and locked up once she got home, she decided to end the chase by ridding herself of the necklace. Deftly removing it from her neck, she flung it in the small canal that ran down the road.

The jeweller, with a cry of anguish, plunged into the canal. So did Rocky. So did I. So did several other people, both adults and children. It was to be a treasure hunt!

Some twenty minutes later, Rocky shouted, 'I've found it!' Covered in mud, water lilies, ferns and tadpoles, we emerged from the canal, and Rocky presented the necklace to the relieved shopkeeper.

Everyone trudged back to the bazaar to find Aunt Ruby waiting in the shop, still trying to make up her mind about a suitable engagement ring.

Finally the ring was bought, the engagement was announced, and a date was set for the wedding.

'I don't want that monkey anywhere near us on our wedding day,' declared Aunt Ruby.

'We'll lock her up in the outhouse,' promised Grandfather. 'And we'll let her out only after you've left for your honeymoon.'

A few days before the wedding I found Tutu in the kitchen,

helping Grandmother prepare the wedding cake. Tutu often helped with the cooking and, when Grandmother wasn't looking, added herbs, spices, and other interesting items to the pots—so that occasionally we found a chilli in the custard or an onion in the jelly or a strawberry floating in the chicken soup.

Sometimes these additions improved a dish, sometimes they did not. Uncle Benji lost a tooth when he bit firmly into a sandwich which contained walnut shells.

I'm not sure exactly what went into that wedding cake when Grandmother wasn't looking—she insisted that Tutu was always very well-behaved in the kitchen—but I did spot Tutu stirring in some red chilli sauce, bitter gourd seeds and a generous helping of egg shells!

It's true that some of the guests were not seen for several days after the wedding, but no one said anything against the cake. Most people thought it had an interesting flavour.

The great day dawned, and the wedding guests made their way to the little church that stood on the outskirts of Dehra—a town with a church, two mosques and several temples.

I had offered to dress Tutu up as a bridesmaid and bring her along, but no one except Grandfather thought it was a good idea. So I was an obedient boy and locked Tutu in the outhouse. I did, however, leave the skylight open a little. Grandmother had always said that fresh air was good for growing children, and I thought Tutu should have her share of it.

◆

The wedding ceremony went without a hitch. Aunt Ruby looked a picture, and Rocky looked like a film star.

Grandfather played the organ, and did so with such gusto that the small choir could hardly be heard. Grandmother cried a little. I sat quietly in a corner, with the little tortoise on my lap.

When the service was over, we trooped out into the sunshine and made our way back to the house for the reception.

The feast had been laid out on tables in the garden. As the gardener had been left in charge, everything was in order. Tutu was on her best behaviour. She had, it appeared, used the skylight to avail of more fresh air outside, and now sat beside the three-tier wedding cake, guarding it against crows, squirrels and the goat. She greeted the guests with squeals of delight.

It was too much for Aunt Ruby. She flew at Tutu in a rage. And Tutu, sensing that she was not welcome, leapt away, taking with her the top tier of the wedding cake.

Led by Major Malik, we followed her into the orchard, only to find that she had climbed to the top of the jackfruit tree. From there she proceeded to pelt us with bits of wedding cake. She had also managed to get hold of a bag of confetti, and when she ran out of cake she showered us with confetti.

'That's more like it!' said the good-humoured Rocky. 'Now let's return to the party, folks!'

Uncle Benji remained with Major Malik, determined to chase Tutu away. He kept throwing stones into the tree, until he received a large piece of cake bang on his nose. Muttering threats, he returned to the party, leaving the major to do battle.

When the festivities were finally over, Uncle Benji took the old car out of the garage and drove up the veranda steps. He was going to drive Aunt Ruby and Rocky to the nearby hill resort of Mussoorie, where they would have their honeymoon.

Watched by family and friends, Aunt Ruby climbed into the back seat. She waved regally to everyone. She leant out of the window and offered me her cheek and I had to kiss her farewell. Everyone wished them luck.

As Rocky burst into song, Uncle Benji opened the throttle and stepped on the accelerator. The car shot forward in a cloud of dust.

Rocky and Aunt Ruby continued to wave to us. And so did Tutu, from her perch on the rear bumper! She was clutching a bag in her hands and showering confetti on all who stood in the driveway.

'They don't know Tutu's with them!' I exclaimed. 'She'll go all the way to Mussoorie! Will Aunt Ruby let her stay with them?'

'Tutu might ruin the honeymoon,' said Grandfather. 'But don't worry—our Benji will bring her back!'

UNCLE KEN GOES BIRDWATCHING

'Where have all the birds gone?' asked Uncle Ken, on a sunny December morning.

At first I thought he was on the subject of a local beauty contest, and I answered, 'To Hollywood, of course, to see Gregory Peck.'

Not being a moviegoer, Uncle Ken missed out on the pun, but he corrected himself and said, 'No, I mean the sparrows. Where have all the sparrows gone?'

This had me baffled. I knew nothing about the sparrows going anywhere, but then, I had never paid much attention to their comings and goings. One is inclined to take sparrows for granted.

'Why do you ask?' I asked.

'Because I've heard they're disappearing. How can we have a world without sparrows?'

'You're thinking of the mountain quail,' I said. 'Sparrows aren't going extinct.'

'Well, I haven't seen any for a long time. And they used to be all over the place. On the veranda steps, at the kitchen window, in the backyard…once, they even made a nest in one of my old hats.'

Uncle Ken had a collection of hats —felt hats, bowler hats, straw hats, floppy hats, pith helmets—and they would lie about in different places and occasionally be forgotten. Three baby mice were discovered in an old bowler hat, a squirrel stored nuts in an old sun helmet; and a small bat made its home in a felt hat that had been hanging too long on the veranda wall.

Uncle Ken seldom went out without a hat of sorts. He did not have much hair on his head and he was afraid of getting sunstroke.

On this particular morning he was wearing a peaked hunting cap, rather like the one used by Sherlock Holmes. It seemed to go with his new-found interest in birds.

'Sparrows,' he repeated. 'What would life be like without sparrows?'

I gave it some thought and said, 'Not very different, I suppose. There would still be other birds.'

'Ah, but would there? If the sparrows go, will the rest be far behind?'

Uncle Ken had a point.

'I would hate to see all the chickens fly away,' I said.

'Why so?'

'Because I like chicken curry.'

'You're just a hedonist, Ruskin. Have you no soul? Imagine a world without beautiful peacocks, swans, nightingales, parakeets, geese, ducks…'

'Granny makes a good duck curry,' I interjected.

'Kingfishers, cranes, seagulls,' continued Uncle Ken.

'We don't get seagulls here,' I said. 'Go back to Pondicherry.'

'All right, then, partridges, cormorants, turkeys...'

'Roast turkey for Christmas. We'll ask Grandfather to get one. And what about crows, Uncle Ken? You've forgotten the crows. You are very popular with them.'

'Plenty of crows about. They are in no danger of extinction. But we have to do something about the sparrows. Where have all the sparrows gone?'

'They've gone next door,' I told him. 'Hadn't you noticed?' And I led him across the garden to the boundary wall, which gave us a clear view of our neighbour's side veranda. There we saw Colonel Mehandru (retired) scattering grain on the veranda steps, while hundreds of sparrows crowded round him, pecking away at the Colonel's largesse.

'A few breadcrumbs won't do,' I told Uncle Ken. 'Buckets of birdseed is what they want. Get some bajra and see the difference!'

So off went Uncle Ken, determined to outdo the Colonel's popularity with the sparrow fraternity. He returned from the bazaar with a sackful of bajra, and began scattering the seeds all over the compound. The squirrels were delighted and so were the hens, but it took some time for the sparrows to reconvert to their former allegiance. Some of them did come over, but as there was plenty of birdseed to be had on the Colonel's side of the wall, there was no great rush to return to our side.

'Is the Colonel's bajra superior to ours?' asked Uncle Ken.

'I'll find out,' I said, and in the afternoon, while the Colonel was taking his siesta, I climbed over the wall, walked up to the veranda steps, and filled my pockets with some of the grain that had been strewn around the place. When I got back to our place, we examined the grain, but were none the wiser; so we consulted Granny.

'It's not bajra,' said Granny. 'That's kangni—it's a smaller seed, easier for small birds to pick up and ingest.'

So off went Uncle Ken again, but he had a hard time finding kangni; the grain merchants did not bother to stock it, as it was strictly for the birds! Apparently Colonel Mehandru had a secret supply.

Not to be discouraged, Uncle Ken continued to scatter bajra in all directions, and soon had a faithful following of pigeons. And this was to lead to his taking up birdwatching in a more ambitious manner.

◆

'These pigeons are all very well,' said Uncle Ken one day. 'But I want to see a green pigeon.'

'Well, I can paint one of these green, if you like,' I offered. 'I'm sure the pigeon won't mind.'

'Don't be an idiot,' said Uncle Ken. 'I want to see the real thing.'

'Are green pigeons very rare, then?'

'Not really. But they are not city birds, like these. They live in trees and don't come down to the ground.'

'What do they live on then?'

'Wild fruit, of course. Berries, etc.'

He'd been reading up Salim Ali's and Whistler's bird books and was showing off his new-found knowledge.

Dhuki, Granny's old gardener, had mentioned that green

pigeons could sometimes be seen in a big banyan tree that grew near Rajpur, at the base of the foothills. It was about five miles from our house.

'Be up early tomorrow,' said Uncle Ken. 'We're going birdwatching. Green pigeons!'

'I was going to play cricket tomorrow morning.'

'Cricket! Such a waste of time. The forest beckons, nature is calling, the wide open spaces are yours to explore—and all you can think of is hitting a ball around the maidan.'

'Actually, I'm a bowler, not a batsman.'

'What could be worse? All that energy spent in flinging a ball at someone who's going to hit it for six anyway!'

It was no use arguing with Uncle Ken—not when he was in the grip of one of his sudden enthusiasms. This was the year of the Bird, as far as he was concerned, and nothing else mattered.

He produced an old pair of binoculars which he had found in the storeroom.

'What are those for?' I asked

'Watching birds, what else?'

I took the binoculars from him and looked them over. 'There's a date stamped here. 1914. Grandfather must have used them in World War I.'

'Well, that shouldn't stop us from using them now.'

I raised them to my eyes and looked out across the garden to where Dhuki was weeding the flower beds. He was just a blur.

'Out of focus,' I said. 'You'll see better without them.'

'We'll take them along anyway. To look more professional.'

◆

Uncle Ken was normally a late riser, but such was his enthusiasm for his new vocation that he was up at the crack of dawn, whistling cheerfully as he turned me out of my bed.

'Up with the lark!' he called. 'Come, listen to the morning thrush!'

'We don't get larks in Dehra,' J said. 'And it's the whistling thrush, not the morning thrush.'

'Well, it's a beautiful morning, and we're going to have a great day. What a lark!'

It didn't take me long to get dressed, but Uncle Ken was ready before me, looking like a Scoutmaster in his shorts (displaying his bandy legs), bush shirt and felt hat with one side turned up quite rakishly.

The bicycles were brought out, and off we went.

'We'll be back in time for breakfast,' said Uncle Ken. He never missed breakfast.

It took us half an hour to reach Rajpur, and the sun was just coming up, sending its shafts of gold through the branches of the great banyan tree that stood outside the village. The tree was alive with birds, and we were free to feast our eyes on parakeets, rosy pastors, bulbuls and other arboreal creatures, but Uncle Ken was determined to locate a green pigeon, and was convinced that he had seen a couple creeping along upside down in the upper branches of the great tree. Handing me the binoculars he proceeded to climb the tree, not too difficult a task, as the banyan has many supporting limbs. I trained the binoculars on the upper branches of the tree, and called out, 'They are not pigeons, Uncle, they're flying foxes!'

Flying foxes are fruit-eating bats, and whole colonies can

sometimes be found in one tree, resting upside down, apparently fast asleep.

But Uncle Ken wasn't listening. He had eyes only for green pigeons, and he ascended the tree until he was in the midst of the roosting flying foxes. They did not take kindly to his sudden appearance. Squeals of anger were followed by a great whirring sound, and scores of bats rose into the air, circling the top of the tree. Two or three swooped down on Uncle Ken, who made a rapid descent, fending off the bats with one arm while clinging to branches with the other. He came down in a most undignified fashion, losing his hat and tearing his shorts. Two of the little creatures were still attached to his collar, and Uncle Ken shouted, 'Knock them off, knock them off!'

I removed them with the help of his hat, and Uncle Ken sat down on the grass and querulously asked, 'Am I bleeding? I think I've been bitten.'

'I don't think so,' I said. 'Just a couple of scratches on your neck.'

'Vampire bats!' moaned Uncle Ken. 'Very infectious. I could go mad!'

I forbore from saying he was already quite mad, but made things even worse by remarking, 'You could become a vampire, Uncle Ken. Like Dracula, you know.'

He went quite pale, gulped, and said, 'Do you really think so, Ruskin?'

'Then you can go around biting people and sucking their blood. What fun!'

'Let's go home,' said Uncle Ken. 'We'll look for the green pigeons another day.'

We returned in time for breakfast, but Uncle Ken barely touched his. He looked very despondent for the rest of the day, and I could see he was very worried about those scratches or bites. I was curious to see if he would develop any of the traits of a vampire, and followed him about wherever he went. On one occasion, I saw him looking speculatively at Aunt Mabel's neck, and I thought he was going to sink his teeth into her flesh. Aunt Mabel a vampire! Now that would have been something. |

But Uncle Ken desisted from biting her, although I could see that he really wanted to. After a few days he recovered his high spirits and began enjoying his breakfast.

Then one day he grabbed me by the arm and said, 'The red jungle fowl, do you know that it's almost extinct? I must see one before it's too late!'

GRANDPA FIGHTS AN OSTRICH

Before my grandfather joined the Indian Railways, he worked for a few years on the East African Railways, and it was during that period that he had his now famous encounter with the ostrich. My childhood was frequently enlivened by this oft-told tale of his, and I give it here in his own words—or as well as I can remember them!

While engaged in the laying of a new railway line, I had a miraculous escape from an awful death. I lived in a small township, but my work lay some twelve miles away, and I had to go to the work site and back on horseback.

One day, my horse had a slight accident, so I decided to do the journey on foot, being a great walker in those days. I also knew of a short cut through the hills that would save me about six miles.

This short cut went through an ostrich farm—or 'camp', as it was called. It was the breeding season. I was fairly familiar with the ways of ostriches, and knew that male birds were very aggressive in the breeding season, ready to attack on the slightest provocation, but I also knew that my dog would scare away any bird that might try to attack me. Strange though it may seem, even the biggest ostrich (and some of them grow to a height of nine feet) will run faster than a racehorse at the sight of even a small dog. So, I felt quite safe in the company of my dog, a mongrel who had adopted me some two months previously.

On arrival at the 'camp', I climbed through the wire fencing and, keeping a good look out, dodged across the open spaces between the thorn bushes. Now and then I caught a glimpse of the birds feeding some distance away.

I had gone about half a mile from the fencing when up started a hare. In an instant my dog gave chase. I tried calling him back, even though I knew it was hopeless. Chasing hares was that dog's passion.

I don't know whether it was the dog's bark or my own shouting, but what I was most anxious to avoid immediately happened. The ostriches were startled and began darting to and fro. Suddenly, I saw a big male bird emerge from a thicket about a hundred yards away. He stood still and stared at me for a few moments. I stared back. Then, expanding his short wings and with his tail erect, he came bounding towards me.

As I had nothing, not even a stick, with which to defend myself, I turned and ran towards the fence. But it was an unequal race. What were my steps of two or three feet against the creature's great strides of sixteen to twenty feet? There was only one hope: to get behind a large bush and try to elude the bird until help came. A dodging game was my only chance.

And so, I rushed for the nearest clump of thorn bushes and waited for my pursuer. The great bird wasted no time—he was immediately upon me.

Then the strangest encounter took place. I dodged this way and that, taking great care not to get directly in front of the ostrich's deadly kick. Ostriches kick forward, and with such terrific force that if you were struck, their huge chisel-like nails would cause you much damage.

I was breathless, and really quite helpless, calling wildly for help as I circled the thorn bush. My strength was ebbing. How much longer could I keep going? I was ready to drop from exhaustion.

As if aware of my condition, the infuriated bird suddenly doubled back on his course and charged straight at me. With a desperate effort I managed to step to one side. I don't know how, but I found myself holding on to one of the creature's wings, quite close to its body.

It was now the ostrich's turn to be frightened. He began to turn, or rather waltz, moving round and round so quickly that my feet were soon swinging out from his body, almost horizontally! All the while the ostrich kept opening and shutting his beak with loud snaps.

Imagine my situation as I clung desperately to the wing of the enraged bird. He was whirling me round and round as though he were a discus-thrower—and I the discus! My arms soon began to ache with the strain, and the swift and continuous circling was making me dizzy. But I knew that if I relaxed my hold, even for a second, a terrible fate awaited me.

Round and round we went in a great circle. It seemed as if that spiteful bird would never tire. And, I knew I could not hold on much longer. Suddenly, the ostrich went into reverse! This unexpected move made me lose my hold and sent me sprawling to the ground. I landed in a heap near the thorn bush and in an instant, before I even had time to realize what had happened, the big bird was upon me. I thought the end had come. Instinctively, I raised my hands to protect my face. But the ostrich did not strike.

I moved my hands from my face and there stood the creature with one foot raised, ready to deliver a deadly kick! I couldn't move. Was the bird going to play cat-and-mouse with me and prolong the agony?

As I watched, frightened and fascinated, the ostrich turned his head sharply to the left. A second later, he jumped back, turned, and made off as fast as he could go. Dazed, I wondered what had happened to make him beat so unexpected a retreat.

I soon found out. To my great joy, I heard the bark of my truant dog, and the next moment he was jumping around me, licking my face and hands. Needless to say, I returned his caresses most affectionately! And I took good care to see that he did not leave my side until we were well clear of that ostrich 'camp'.

A TIGER IN THE HOUSE

Timothy, the tiger cub, was discovered by Grandfather on a hunting expedition in the Terai jungle near Dehra.

Grandfather was no shikari, but as he knew the forests of the Siwalik hills better than most people, he was persuaded to accompany the party—it consisted of several Very Important Persons from Delhi—to advise on the terrain and the direction the beaters should take once a tiger had been spotted.

The camp itself was sumptuous—seven large tents (one for each shikari), a dining tent and a number of servants' tents. The dinner was very good, as Grandfather admitted afterwards; it was not often that one saw hot-water plates, finger glasses and seven or eight courses in a tent in the jungle! But that was how things were done in the days of the viceroys... There were also some fifteen elephants, four of them with howdahs for the shikaris, and the others specially trained for taking part in the beat.

The sportsmen never saw a tiger, nor did they shoot anything else, though they saw a number of deer, peacock and wild boar. They were giving up all hope of finding a tiger and were beginning to shoot at jackals, when Grandfather, strolling down the forest path at some distance from the rest of the party, discovered a little tiger about eighteen inches long, hiding among the intricate roots of a banyan tree. Grandfather picked him up and brought him home after the camp had broken up. He had the distinction of being the only member of the party to have bagged any game, dead or alive.

At first the tiger cub, who was named Timothy by Grandmother, was brought up entirely on milk given to him in a feeding bottle by our cook, Mahmoud. But the milk proved too rich for him, and he was put on a diet of raw mutton and cod liver oil, to be followed later by a more tempting diet of pigeons and rabbits.

Timothy was provided with two companions—Toto the monkey, who was bold enough to pull the young tiger by the tail, and then climb up the curtains if Timothy lost his temper; and a small mongrel puppy, found on the road by Grandfather.

At first Timothy appeared to be quite afraid of the puppy and darted back with a spring if it came too near. He would make absurd dashes at it with his large forepaws and then retreat to a ridiculously safe distance. Finally, he allowed the puppy to crawl on his back and rest there!

One of Timothy's favourite amusements was to stalk anyone who would play with him, and so, when I came to live with Grandfather, I became one of the tiger's favourites. With a crafty look in his glittering eyes, and his body crouching, he would creep closer and closer to me, suddenly making a dash for my feet, rolling over on his back and kicking with delight, and pretending to bite my ankles.

He was by this time the size of a full-grown retriever, and when I took him out for walks, people on the road would give us a wide berth. When he pulled hard on his chain, I had difficulty in keeping up with him. His favourite place in the house was the drawing room, and he would make himself comfortable on the long sofa, reclining there with great dignity and snarling at anybody who tried to get him off.

Timothy had clean habits, and would scrub his face with his paws exactly like a cat. At night, he slept in the cook's quarters and was always delighted at being let out by him in the morning.

'One of these days,' declared Grandmother in her prophetic manner, 'we are going to find Timothy sitting on Mahmoud's bed, and no sign of the cook except his clothes and shoes!'

Of course, it never came to that, but when Timothy was about six months old a change came over him; he grew steadily less friendly. When out for a walk with me, he would try to steal away to stalk a cat or someone's pet Pekingese. Sometimes at night we would hear frenzied cackling from the poultry house, and in the morning there would be feathers lying all over the veranda. Timothy had to be chained up more often. And, finally, when he began to stalk Mahmoud about the house with what looked like villainous intent, Grandfather decided it was time to transfer him to a zoo.

The nearest zoo was at Lucknow, two hundred miles away. Reserving a first-class compartment for himself and Timothy— no one would share a compartment with them—Grandfather took him to Lucknow where the zoo authorities were only too glad to receive as a gift a well-fed and fairly civilized tiger.

About six months later, when my grandparents were visiting relatives in Lucknow, Grandfather took the opportunity of calling at the zoo to see how Timothy was getting on. I was not there to accompany him, but I heard all about it when he returned to Dehra.

Arriving at the zoo, Grandfather made straight for the particular cage in which Timothy had been interned. The tiger was there, crouched in a corner, full-grown and with a magnificent striped coat.

'Hello, Timothy!' said Grandfather and, climbing the railing with ease, he put his arm through the bars of the cage.

The tiger approached the bars and allowed Grandfather to put both hands around his head. Grandfather stroked the tiger's forehead and tickled his ear, and, whenever he growled, smacked him across the mouth, which was his old way of keeping him quiet.

He licked Grandfather's hands and only sprang away when a leopard in the next cage snarled at him. Grandfather 'shooed' the leopard away and the tiger returned to lick his hands; but every now and then the leopard would rush at the bars and the tiger would slink back to his corner.

A number of people had gathered to watch the reunion when a keeper pushed his way through the crowd and asked Grandfather what he was doing.

'I'm talking to Timothy,' said Grandfather. 'Weren't you here when I gave him to the zoo six months ago?'

'I haven't been here very long,' said the surprised keeper. 'Please continue your conversation. But I have never been able to touch him myself, he is always very bad tempered.'

'Why don't you put him somewhere else?' suggested Grandfather. 'That leopard keeps frightening him. I'll go and see the superintendent about it.'

Grandfather went in search of the superintendent of the zoo, but found that he had gone home early; and so, after wandering about the zoo for a little while, he returned to Timothy's cage to say goodbye. It was beginning to get dark.

He had been stroking and slapping Timothy for about five minutes when he found another keeper observing him with some alarm. Grandfather recognized him as the keeper who had been there when Timothy had first come to the zoo.

'*You* remember me,' said Grandfather. 'Now why don't you transfer Timothy to another cage, away from this stupid leopard?'

'But—sir—' stammered the keeper, 'it is not your tiger.'

'I know, I know,' said Grandfather testily. 'I realize he is no longer mine. But you might at least take a suggestion or two from me.'

'I remember your tiger very well,' said the keeper. 'He died two months ago.'

'Died!' exclaimed Grandfather.

'Yes, sir, of pneumonia. This tiger was trapped in the hills only last month, and he is very dangerous!'

Grandfather could think of nothing to say. The tiger was still licking his arm, with increasing relish. Grandfather took what seemed to him an age to withdraw his hand from the cage.

With his face near the tiger's he mumbled, 'Goodnight, Timothy,' and giving the keeper a scornful look, walked briskly out of the zoo.

MAN AND LEOPARD

I first saw the leopard when I was crossing the small stream at the bottom of the hill.

The ravine was so deep that for most of the day it remained in shadow. This encouraged many birds and animals to emerge from cover during the daylight hours. Few people ever passed that way: only milkmen and charcoal burners from the surrounding villages. As a result, the ravine had become a little haven for wildlife, one of the few natural sanctuaries left near Mussoorie, a hill station in northern India.

Below my cottage was a forest of oak and maple and Himalayan rhododendron. A narrow path twisted its way down through the trees, over an open ridge where red sorrel grew wild, and then steeply down through a tangle of wild raspberries, creeping vines and slender bamboo. At the bottom of the hill the path led on to a grassy verge, surrounded by wild dog roses. (It is surprising how closely the flora of the lower Himalayas, between 5,000 and 8,000 feet, resembles that of the English countryside.)

The stream ran close by the verge, tumbling over smooth pebbles, over rocks worn yellow with age, on its way to the plains and to the little Song River and finally to the sacred Ganga.

When I first discovered the stream, it was early April and the wild roses were flowering—small white blossoms lying in clusters.

I walked down to the stream almost every day after two or three hours of writing. I had lived in cities too long and had returned to the hills to renew myself, both physically and mentally. Once you have lived with mountains for any length of time you belong to them, and must return again and again.

Nearly every morning, and sometimes during the day, I heard the cry of the barking deer. And in the evening, walking through the forest, I disturbed parties of pheasants. The birds went gliding down the ravine on open, motionless wings. I saw pine martens and a handsome red fox, and I recognized the footprints of a bear.

As I had not come to take anything from the forest, the birds and animals soon grew accustomed to my presence; or possibly they recognized my footsteps. After some time, my approach did not disturb them.

The langurs in the oak and rhododendron trees, who would at first go leaping through the branches at my approach, now watched me with some curiosity as they munched the tender green shoots of the oak. The young ones scuffled and wrestled like boys while their parents groomed each other's coats, stretching themselves out on the sunlit hillside.

But one evening, as I passed, I heard them chattering in the trees, and I knew I was not the cause of their excitement. As I crossed the stream and began climbing the hill, the grunting and chattering increased, as though the langurs were trying to warn me of some hidden danger. A shower of pebbles came rattling down the steep hillside, and I looked up to see a sinewy, orange-gold leopard poised on a rock about twenty feet above me.

He was not looking towards me but had his head thrust attentively forward, in the direction of the ravine. Yet he must have sensed my presence, because he slowly turned his head and looked down at me.

He seemed a little puzzled at my presence there; and when, to give myself courage, I clapped my hands sharply, the leopard sprang away into the thickets, making absolutely no sound as he melted into the shadows.

I had disturbed the animal in his quest for food. But a little after I heard the quickening cry of a barking deer as it fled through the forest. The hunt was still on.

The leopard, like other members of the cat family, is nearing extinction in India, and I was surprised to find one so close to Mussoorie. Probably the deforestation that had been taking place in the surrounding hills had driven the deer into this green valley; and the leopard, naturally, had followed.

It was some weeks before I saw the leopard again, although I was often made aware of its presence. A dry, rasping cough sometimes gave it away. At times I felt almost certain that I was being followed.

Once, when I was late getting home, and the brief twilight gave way to a dark moonless night, I was startled by a family of porcupines running about in a clearing. I looked around nervously and saw two bright eyes staring at me from a thicket. I stood still, my heart banging away against my ribs. Then the eyes danced away and I realized that they were only fireflies.

In May and June, when the hills were brown and dry, it was always cool and green near the stream, where ferns and maidenhair and long grasses continued to thrive.

Downstream, I found a small pool where I could bathe, and a cave with water dripping from the roof, the water spangled gold and silver in the shafts of sunlight that pushed through the slits in the cave roof.

'He maketh me to lie down in green pastures; he leadeth me beside the still waters.' Perhaps David had discovered a similar paradise when he wrote those words; perhaps I, too, would write good words. The hill station's summer visitors had not discovered this haven of wild and green things. I was beginning to feel that the place belonged to me, that dominion was mine.

The stream had at least one other regular visitor, a spotted forktail, and though it did not fly away at my approach, it became restless if I stayed too long, and then she would move from boulder to boulder uttering a long complaining cry.

I spent an afternoon trying to discover the bird's nest, which I was certain contained young ones, because I had seen the forktail carrying grubs in her bill. The problem was that when the bird flew upstream, I had difficulty in following her rapidly enough as the rocks were sharp and slippery.

Eventually I decorated myself with bracken fronds and, after slowly making my way upstream, hid myself in the hollow stump of a tree at a spot where the forktail often disappeared. I had no intention of robbing the bird. I was simply curious to see its home.

By crouching down, I was able to command a view of a small stretch of the stream and the side of the ravine; but I had done little to deceive the forktail, who continued to object strongly to my presence so near her home.

I summoned up my reserves of patience and sat perfectly still for about ten minutes. The forktail quietened down. Out of sight, out of mind. But where had she gone? Probably into the walls of the ravine where, I felt sure, she was guarding her nest.

I decided to take her by surprise and stood up suddenly, in time to see not the forktail on her doorstep but the leopard bounding away with a grunt of surprise! Two urgent springs, and he had crossed the stream and plunged into the forest.

I was as astonished as the leopard, and forgot all about the forktail and her nest. Had the leopard been following me again? I decided against this possibility. Only man-eaters follow humans and, as far as I knew, there had never been a man-eater in the vicinity of Mussoorie.

During the monsoon the stream became a rushing torrent; bushes and small trees were swept away, and the friendly murmur of the water became a threatening boom. I did not visit the place too often as there were leeches in the long grass.

One day I found the remains of a barking deer, which had only been partly eaten. I wondered why the leopard had not hidden the rest of his meal, and decided that it must have been disturbed while eating.

Then, climbing the hill, I met a party of hunters resting beneath the oaks. They asked me if I had seen a leopard. I said I had not. They said they knew there was a leopard in the forest.

Leopard skins, they told me, were selling in Delhi at over a thousand rupees each. Of course there was a ban on the export of skins, but they gave me to understand that there were ways and means… I thanked them for their information and walked on, feeling uneasy and disturbed.

The hunters had seen the carcass of the deer, and they had seen the leopard's pug marks, and they kept coming to the forest. Almost every evening I heard their guns banging away; for they were ready to fire at almost anything.

'There's a leopard about,' they always told me. 'You should carry a gun.'

'I don't have one,' I said.

There were fewer birds to be seen, and even the langurs had moved on. The red fox did not show itself; and the pine martens, who had become quite bold, now dashed into hiding at my approach. The smell of one human is like the smell of any other.

And then the rains were over and it was October. I could lie in the sun, on sweet-smelling grass, and gaze up through a pattern of oak leaves into a blinding blue heaven. And I would praise God for leaves and grass and the smell of things—the smell of mint and bruised clover—and the touch of things—the touch of grass and air and sky, the touch of the sky's blueness.

I thought no more of the men. My attitude towards them was similar to that of the denizens of the forest. These were men, unpredictable, and to be avoided if possible.

On the other side of the ravine rose Pari Tibba, Hill of the Fairies; a bleak, scrub-covered hill where no one lived.

It was said that in the previous century Englishmen had tried building their houses on the hill, but the area had always attracted lightning, due to either the hill's location or due to its mineral deposits; after several houses had been struck by lightning, the settlers had moved on to the next hill, where the town now stands.

To the hillmen it is Pari Tibba, haunted by the spirits of a pair of ill-fated lovers who perished there in a storm; to others it is known as Burnt Hill, because of its scarred and stunted trees.

One day, after crossing the stream, I climbed Pari Tibba—a stiff undertaking, because there was no path to the top and I had to scramble up a precipitous rock face with the help of rocks and roots that were apt to come loose in my groping hands.

But at the top was a plateau with a few pine trees, their upper branches catching the wind and humming softly. There I found the ruins of what must have been the houses of the first settlers—just a few piles of rubble, now overgrown with weeds, sorrel, dandelions and nettles.

As I walked though the roofless ruins, I was struck by the silence that surrounded me, the absence of birds and animals, the sense of complete desolation.

The silence was so absolute that it seemed to be ringing in my ears. But there was something else of which I was becoming increasingly aware: the strong feline odour of one of the cat family. I paused and looked about. I was alone. There was no movement of dry leaf or loose stone.

The ruins were for the most part open to the sky. Their rotting rafters had collapsed, jamming together to form a low passage like the entrance to a mine; and this dark cavern seemed to lead down into the ground. The smell was stronger when I approached this spot, so I stopped again and waited there, wondering if I had discovered the lair of the leopard, wondering if the animal was now at rest after a night's hunt.

Perhaps he was crouching there in the dark, watching me,

104 • *Grandfather's Private Zoo*

recognizing me, knowing me as the man who walked alone in the forest without a weapon.

I like to think that he was there, that he knew me, and that he acknowledged my visit in the friendliest way: by ignoring me altogether.

Perhaps I had made him confident—too confident, too careless, too trusting of the human in his midst. I did not venture any further; I was not out of my mind. I did not seek physical contact, or even another glimpse of that beautiful sinewy body, springing from rock to rock. It was his trust I wanted, and I think he gave it to me.

But did the leopard, trusting one man, make the mistake of bestowing his trust on others? Did I, by casting out all fear—my own fear, and the leopard's protective fear—leave him defenceless?

Because the next day, coming up the path from the stream, shouting and beating drums, were the hunters. They had a long bamboo pole across their shoulders; and slung from the pole, feet up, head down, was the lifeless body of the leopard, shot in the neck and in the head.

'We told you there was a leopard!' they shouted, in great good humour. 'Isn't he a fine specimen?'

'Yes,' I said. 'He was a beautiful leopard.'

I walked home through the silent forest. It was very silent, almost as though the birds and animals knew that their trust had been violated.

I remembered the lines of a poem by D.H. Lawrence; and, as I climbed the steep and lonely path to my home, the words beat out their rhythm in my mind: 'There was room in the world for a mountain lion and me.'

www.ingramcontent.com/pod-product-compliance
Lightning Source LLC
Chambersburg PA
CBHW020025030726
47499CB00007B/2277